I0616862

Surgeons of Terror 5

Yar Island

Ron Wootters

"Surgeons of Terror 5—Yar Island," by Ron Wootters. ISBN 978-1-60264-257-7.

Published 2008 by Virtualbookworm.com Publishing Inc., P.O. Box 9949, College Station, TX 77842, US. ©2008, Ron Wootters. All rights reserved. No part of this publication may be reproduced, stored in a retrieval system, or transmitted in any form or by any means, electronic, mechanical, recording or otherwise, without the prior written permission of Ron Wootters.

Manufactured in the United States of America.

To:

**All U.S. Intelligence and Armed Forces
Personnel
Past, Present & Future.
Thank You.**

Edited by:
Lisa DiGloria
Book Ink Editing
www.bookink.com

In Memory Of:

**All coalition personnel who lost their lives
serving their countries in
Iraq or Afghanistan**

Continued Special Thanks To The Medical Community:
Dr. David DiPietro, M.D. Family Practice
Dr. Paul Spiro, M.D. Family Practice
Dr. Joseph Curci, M.D. General Surgery
Dr. Bruce Derrick M.D. General Surgery
Dr. Bruce Applestein M.D. Cardiology
Dr. Michael Mooradd, M.D. Cardiology
Dr. Steven Guidera, M.D. Cardiology
Dr. Randy Metcalf, M.D. Cardiothoracic Surgery
Dr. Joseph Auteri M.D. Cardiothoracic Surgery
Dr. James H. Wright M.D. Anesthesiology
Dr. Robert O'Connor M.D. Anesthesiology
Dr. Jon Walheim M.D. Internal Medicine
Dr. Joseph Shrager, M.D. Dermatology
Dr. June E. Grutzmacher M.D. Ophthalmology
Dr. Steven Flashner, M.D. Urology
Dr. Melchiore Vernace, M.D. Nephrology
Dr. Timothy Orphanides, M.D. Gastroenterology
Dr. Frank A. Welsch M.D. Pulmonary Disease
Dr. Les Szekely, M.D. Pulmonary Disease
Dr. Stanford Gittlen M.D. Pulmonary Disease
Dr. Richard Rathgeber D.O. Emergency Medicine
Dr. Robert Linkenheimer, D.O. Emergency Medicine
Dr. Mark Choi, M.D. Emergency Medicine
Dr. Lawrence Brilliant M.D. Emergency Medicine
Dr. Mark Bydalek, D.M.D Dentistry
Dr. Lynn M. Azzara M.P.D Podiatry
Dr. Douglas Boylan M.D. Orthopaedic Surgery
Dr. J. Michael Whitaker M.D. Orthopaedic Surgery
Dr. Daniel J. Coletta M.D. Gynecology
Dr. Laurie Gerstein M.D. Gynecology
Dr. Douglas Nadel M.D. Otolaryngology
Dr. Elana Eisner M.D. Rheumatology
Emergency Department Doylestown Hospital
The Heart Institute Doylestown Hospital
The Cath Lab Doylestown Hospital
Cardiac Rehab Center Doylestown Hospital.
Physician Assistant's, Labs, Nurses, Staff, Mr. Rich Reif
and the Board of Directors at Doylestown Hospital

To All Good Nurses Everywhere.

Lambertville—New Hope Ambulance and Rescue Squad
When the siren calls the Squad is already on the way

Doctors, PA's, Nurses and Staffs at:
Buckingham Family Medicine
Joseph J. Curci, M.D., F.A.C.S.
Central Bucks Cardiology
Bucks County Cardiothoracic Surgery
New Hope-Solebury Dermatology
Central Bucks Urology
Nephrology-Hypertension Specialist
Central Bucks Specialists Limited
Mark Bydalek, DMD
Bucks County Medical Association / Pulmonary
June E. Grutzmacher, M.D., F.A.C.S.
Doylestown Orthopedic Specialists
Doylestown Internal Medicine
Doylestown Gynecology
Ent Associates of Bucks County
Rheumatology Specialty Center
Lynn M. Azzara, MPD

Rosemary and I are very fortunate to live in an area where
we have access to such excellent medical care.

PROLOGUE

The devil's den during Christmas week, what's wrong with this picture?, Gil Dunn thought to himself, as he pulled to the side of the road in Gettysburg National Military Park not far from a clump of huge boulders that stood out from the rest of the landscape. *Di Flippi is either working on his sense of humor or he is going to tell me something really bad.* Dunn continued to wonder as he got out of his car and walked toward the boulders.

The Battlefield had become their meeting place whenever Di wanted to discuss a very serious matter with his old boss at the Agency.

Gil was glad to help his old friend and after their first meeting when things happened unexpectedly to solve the problem, Di Flippi realized Dunn was the go to guy if he had a very serious problem that couldn't be solved due to bureaucrats or politics at the CIA.

Di had parked his car further up the road, walked back to the rock formation, and was waiting as Gil approached.

"It's colder than a rat's ass out here. Couldn't this wait until after spring thaw?" Dunn inquired.

"Afraid not," Di replied.

"I knew you were going to say that," Dunn confirmed, as the two men walked to the huge boulders and found some protection against the cold north wind.

Di produced two Cuban cigars and after being reprimanded by Dunn for offering him contraband, the two lit them up and took a long puff on the fine cigars, then slowly exhaled.

"One of the few enjoyments I get these days," Di said with a smile.

"They are an excellent smoke," Dunn agreed.

After another puff on his cigar, Dunn inquired, "I'm starting to feel like the proverbial brass monkey. Do we have something to discuss?"

"No," Di replied, "just wanted to wish you a Merry Christmas."

"That's funny," Gil acknowledged. "You are working on your sense of humor."

The two men smiled then Di Flippi started to tell Dunn the real reason he asked to see him. "Have another very serious matter that needs to be addressed, but yet again have hit that bureaucratic stonewall." Di explained. "Have Intel from way inside the terrorist network about a plan to set off explosives inside an Amtrak passenger train during morning rush hour as it passes under the Hudson River on its way to Penn Station in New York City.

"I have the date, time, and hope to get some ID on the bombers very soon. My problem is that the higher-ups want to know my exact source of Intel and let's just say in that timeframe years ago when you were the DDO at the Agency, I had no problems with sharing the source of any type of Intel, but these days, it's pick and choose when it comes to very, very sensitive material."

For the first time since they started having their meetings, Dunn was not a happy camper. When they started meeting shortly after 9/11, Dunn could sort of understand why Di was having these problems. Due to uncertainty and getting organized to fight the new fight, higher-ups were probably apprehensive about making certain decisions, but over six years had passed and the same problems still existed.

"So you want us to intervene again and on U.S. soil?" Dunn inquired with a serious voice.

The two men never really talked in those terms, but rather in vague references and Di was taken back by Gil's reply.

"I was hoping," Di Flippi answered.

"I'm not directing any anger toward you," Gil informed

Di Flippi. "I know you are just trying to do your job and in the process save lives, but these assholes that work their way up the chain by playing politics piss me off and maybe somebody needs a lesson."

"If you're saying what I think you're saying, it would be a very costly lesson," Di Flippi observed.

"Maybe that's what they need," Gil fired back. "Besides, executing missions on U.S. soil puts our group at added risks and the scrutiny of federal law enforcement. Think I'll have to pass on this one," Dunn finished.

Di Flippi sat quietly pondering Dunn's words then said, "Maybe you're right, Gil. Maybe they do need a wakeup call."

CHAPTER ONE

J J Stone gave a long look at each man seated around the conference table as they talked among themselves prior to the meeting being called to order.

General Mac, USMC retired; John Howard, president of Zerk Pharmaceutical; Jeff Dawson, president of International Oil; Gil Dunn, president of Van Corcoven Firearms Company and former DDO at CIA; Admiral Fox (Foxie), Navy retired; and Charles Wilson, president of Wilson Explosives Company.

In 2001, JJ had recruited these men to serve on a board that would finance and oversee projects aimed at the destruction of terrorist elements around the world. Teams were formed and both terrorist and narco/terrorist groups had been eliminated.

After the 9/11 attacks, the projects had become bigger and more dangerous stretching the

Board and Teams to their max, but no one ever complained.

For the first item on today's agenda, JJ would propose the Board and Teams be dissolved for two reasons. One, they had been very lucky for over seven years with no fatalities and the one security breach they had early on was taken care of before any damage was done. Two, was there really a need for them to continue due to less terrorist activity these days?

This was a bittersweet proposal for JJ. Bitter because he enjoyed being around and working with his old friends on the Board and his new friends on the Teams, and he would miss that very much. It was sweet because he was responsible for forming the group and was constantly concerned about the welfare of everyone, especially each time they took on a new Project. For the Board, it could mean ruin and prison, but for the Teams and on occasion the Board members themselves, it could be far worse.

JJ was still in deep thought when he heard Mac say, "You have that look again."

"What look?" JJ replied, as the Board members listened in.

"That look you get when you're concerned about everyone's well being."

"We're not going through that shit again, are we?" Howard inquired.

"Well, since you people have brought it up, yes, we are," JJ advised everyone, as he sat up straight and called the meeting to order.

After JJ presented the proposal, it was discussed in great length with each member expressing his opinion on the matter. It ended with Dawson saying, "If a liberal president takes office in 2009, terrorist activities could become very active again."

The opinions expressed were very convincing and when JJ called for a vote, even he voted in favor of continuing with the Projects making it unanimous.

"If you people are sure about this, I guess the next item will be a review of the last Project."

Everyone shook their heads in agreement, so JJ went into his briefcase and distributed folders to the other members.

"In past post-Project meetings, we have included a review of the Teams and I feel it may be a good time to conduct another quick run-through. I'll read each Team member's codename and primary expertise, and you can ask questions or make comments at that time." All agreed and JJ continued. "Team Leader, JC, retired Marine Corps Colonel, pilot, expert with weapons, and our main gizmo man. Blue Jay, field Team Leader, contract type, former Marine Corps and CIA. Bean, contract type, prior Army Airborne Ranger, Special Forces, and CIA. Benz, Japanese, expert in martial arts, been in the contract business part-time for many years. Panda, Philippino, also martial arts, part-time contractor, regular occupation: engineering consultant. Check, Arab, explosives, part-time contractor, owns a Middle East restaurant. Tic, Cuban, explosives, part-time contractor, regular occupation: stockbroker. Bris, French, primarily a contractor, but also an artist and a good one, too. Pru, English, contractor, long-range shooter. Met, German, also a contractor, long-range shooter. Air Jockey, contractor, can fly helicopters, most prop aircraft, the corporate jet, and able to function as a Team member on the ground if needed."

"Have a question," Foxie interrupted, raising his hand.

"Jockey has a full boat just flying the helicopter and corporate jet. Do we want to keep putting him in harm's way with the Team?"

"Last time JC and I asked Jockey about maybe cutting back, he got a little put out about being excluded from Team ops," Mac spoke up, "so we decided instead of excluding him from Team ground activities, we would get more depth in the flying department.

"From the beginning, JC has been the backup for prop aircraft, helicopter, and has added the corporate jet. In addition to that, I am also a backup for prop aircraft and corporate jet, and as you all know, Dawson is also qualified to pilot corporate jets."

"I'll check with him again to see if anything has changed," Mac assured Foxie who shook his head in agreement.

"Now for the House Team." JJ continued the review.

"Top Kiner, retired 1st Sergeant Marine Corps. Lady1 and LadyA, former Intelligence field operatives. The House Teams primary responsibilities are home base and as you all know, they have been active participants during past Projects and I have a feeling that trend will continue. Are there any questions or comments?"

It went without saying the Board members were still more than satisfied with the Teams' performances and they all remained silent.

"That concludes the reviews of the Teams, now we'll move on to our three relatively new members, Jar Head, Doggie, and Swabbie," JJ announced. "As you all know, they joined our ranks after the House Team foiled a kidnapping and assassination attempt by Al-Qaida and have been a great contribution to our efforts. Prior to that, they were in retirement and I would like your opinions on how to proceed. Should I approach them about going back into retirement or let things take their course? I don't want to insult them, but at the same time, I don't want them to feel obligated to stay active."

"Have they said anything that suggests they would like to go back into retirement?" Foxie inquired.

"Not really," JJ answered.

"Maybe it would be best to approach all three when they are together and ask what they have in mind," Dawson suggested.

"I guess the direct approach would be the best," JJ agreed. "They are still staying at the main house until their new houses are built, so I will check with them first thing tomorrow morning."

With that item resolved, JJ moved on. "Now for the medical support area. Dr. D, MD and Dr. C, surgeon, are still onboard.

"With two years of med school in his background, Check has been the field medic since the Team was formed. Bris and Tic, with the help of the doctors and Check, are now up to speed and can serve as paramedics if needed.

"What we all now refer to as The Medevac-Jet is still made ready when a Project goes operational. The jet is equipped with an operating theatre and can fly the doctors to a planned location if needed.

"We have not required medical assistance in the past and let's all pray we don't need it in the future," JJ commented.

"Amen to that," Mac added with a sincere voice.

"Now onto the financial matters," JJ said and all Board members reached for their briefcases.

Financial planning was the last item on the agenda and would take hours to complete before JJ would adjourn the meeting.

The meeting had gone on for some time when JJ said, "I think it's time for a coffee," and everyone agreed.

After returning to the conference table with their coffees, the Board members engaged in small talk before returning to the financial planning.

"I wonder where the Team members went for furlough," Dawson wondered aloud.

"I don't know," Mac replied, "but when they return, training will be the first thing on their agenda. When the Team was first formed and before the first Project was executed, JC started what he called, *Lock on training* for a period of time to get everyone into the same condition. At that time, someone in the group commented, *Lock on this,* but I guess after a while, they thought it was a good idea and have continued to do it on their own every time they return from furlough. The morning after they return, they will be running, lifting weights, and practicing martial arts, just for starters."

The Board members all smiled after hearing Mac's report, then Wilson inquired, "Mac, have you ever practiced any martial arts?"

"When I was in the Corps. Every time I was stationed in North Carolina used to practice judo with Sergeant Smith at the Camp Lejeune Judo Club. How about yourself?"

"Used to practice judo as well at the Karate and Judo Center in Cranford, New Jersey. The chief instructor was a 7th degree black belt named Mr. Yonezuka, but everyone called him Yone. They have a saying in this country, 'Those that can't play, teach,' but that couldn't be further from the truth when it came to Yone. He was a champion in Japan and the U.S., was the U.S. Olympic Judo coach twice, and many of his students were also champions. He was so fast you never saw a throw coming until you were already in the air."

"Sounds like Benz, doesn't it, Mac?" JJ asked and Mac agreed.

"I used to workout with a 4th degree named Andy Domingo a lot." Wilson continued. "Both he and Yone would give you a chance to practice your offensive skills, but sooner or later, you knew you were going to take a ride in the air."

The Board members chuckled and Wilson said, "How about you, Dawson?"

"Yes, it was years ago, but I still have good memories about those days. I used to travel to Philly and train at the Philadelphia Karate Club. Those were great times. Mr. Okazaki was a 7th degree black belt and chief instructor. Mr. Enoeda was a 5th and Mr. Kisaka a 4th degree. Both had been champions in Japan and had been Mr. Okazaki's students in Japan, too. In addition to being champions, all were excellent instructors and during some classes, all three would be instructing. It just didn't get much better than that. Now Mr. Okazaki is still in Philadelphia, Mr. Kisaka is in Trenton, New Jersey, and Mr. Enoeda passed on a few years ago. It was just one of those times when things all came together and I was fortunate enough to be there."

The Board members made comments about the conversations then got quiet.

"Mac, I can't get over that you played judo, too," Wilson commented. "So at your weight class, did they make you workout with the girls?"

"Ding!" JJ said in a loud voice before the reply he knew was coming from Mac. "Gil, I think we may have set a new record for civil conversation."

"Just barely," Dunn agreed, as he checked his watch.

While he had an opening, JJ called the meeting back to order. Between the coffee, laughter, and adrenaline, they would get off to a fresh start.

JJ had gotten home late from the Board meeting the night before and didn't show up in the kitchen until about eight A.M.

"Good afternoon," Top and the Ladies greeted him. "The usual?" Top inquired about morning breakfast.

"Yes, please," JJ replied, then inquired, "Are Jar Head, Doggie, and Swabbie still in the area?"

"No." Top Kiner replied. "As usual, they were up at dawn for breakfast then left on morning recon patrol to the building sites."

"Have you lived here long?" LadyA inquired.

"Maybe he hit his head or something?" Lady1 added.

"That was a dumb question wasn't it?" JJ admitted with a chuckle. The three men in question had the same morning routine since they started breaking ground for their three new houses. "Well, it's early and I had a late night," he defended.

After breakfast, JJ drove the short distance to the building sites. He had sold them a wooded area on his land for one dollar and they in turn had divided it into three building lots. JJ had not visited the building sites yet, but after listening to the discussions between Blue Jay, Bean, and their old mentors, security seemed to be the primary considerations from day one.

These discussions started after the duo reviewed the building plans and Blue Jay inquired, *Are you worried about Indian attacks?* and before the three could respond, Bean added, *You do know*

*the Delaware Indians aren't around here any-
more, don't you?*

Things went downhill from there and after
that, the discussions usually broke out on a daily
basis.

Everyone, especially Blue Jay and Bean,
knew the houses were very important to the three
men and everyone would make inspection visits
during the building process, but for now, the daily
discussions usually started with something like,
*Why don't you put a high fence around the three
lots and call it Fort something?* Usually followed
with something like, *How about Fort Old Farts?*

———————

For construction of the houses, JJ had put Jar
Head, Doggie, and Swabbie in touch with local
businesses he had used in the past and a few new
ones, too.

Carpenters Dan Di Salvi's team, Tony Denise
and his crew, and John Wicks. Joe Altvater and
his four sons for the roofing. Plumbing would be
done by John Hoff's group. The electricians Brian
Fitting and Fred Nanni. Painters Dave Stryker and
Michael Williams. Masons Ben Andersen, Brian
Slack & company were hired. Excavation was
done by Roy Myers, Jeff Lawson, and George
Kilmer with the Shearer Penn Tree Company
trimming or removing trees on the three adjoining
lots. Charles (Spooky) Rose and Tom Briggs were
also coaxed out of retirement to add their expertise
to the projects.

Always good work done by good people.

As JJ pulled into the temporary lane used by the contractors, he spotted Jar Head, Doggie, and Swabbie checking out one of the foundations being dug and he headed in their direction. The three men saw JJ turn into the lane and were waiting as he brought his Jaguar to a stop.

As he opened the car door and was in the process of getting out, Doggie asked, "Come to check out the fort?"

"Yeah, that, too," JJ answered with a smile.

After offering each man a cigar and requesting a tour of the area, the four men started walking and talking. The group stopped by the third lot and watched as limbs were secured, then cut, and lowered to the ground by a small crane.

"Look at that guy," Doggie said, as he pointed to a man rappelling from a rope and swinging from limb to limb, as he trimmed the top of a giant oak tree.

"He's having way too much fun," Jar Head observed and the others agreed with a chuckle.

As they continued to watch, the three men explained to JJ that for security reasons, the houses were positioned so from each house, one could at least see the front and back of one of the others and how they incorporated the existing trees into their plan so nothing would look odd or out of place.

"That's not a bad idea," JJ approved, and then added, "Let me guess, that's the reason for the name 'Fort Old Farts'?"

"It gets better than that," Swabbie quickly answered. "The duo that is giving us the most grief about it helped developed the plans."

"Blue Jay and Bean," JJ said, then started to laugh after Swabbie confirmed it with a headshake.

"Did you ever think about revealing that fact during your daily discussions?" JJ suggested.

"No fun in doing that," Jar Head replied.

"Besides, now we know what the topic will be and prepare for it. If we reveal the facts, they would move onto something else and we would have to spend more time to prepare."

JJ was still laughing as he looked at Swabbie who said, "This is nothing. You should have seen the shit I had to put up with when they all worked for me at the Agency. Ask Dunn, he'll tell you."

After that statement, the other two started laughing. "Remember all of those times Dunn threatened to fire us?"

Doggie asked Jar Head.

"Remember all of those occasions when we were in the middle when he wanted to fire Bean and Blue Jay?"

"How about the time he was so pissed off he even threatened them with prison," was the reply and that memory made Swabbie burst into laughter as well.

When the three had finished their laugh, JJ brought up the reason for his visit. "We had a Board meeting yesterday and in the process, reviewed our T.O. You three have been a great contribution to our efforts and the question was asked if you are planning to continue with us or go back into retirement?"

"We have already discussed this and if it were just the three of us, we would be in it full-time, but our wives have dealt with us being in harm's way for a long time and deserve this time with us," Swabbie replied.

"Let me qualify that," Jar Head spoke up. "We will always be available for the planning stage of a project, but have decided to stay out of the field ops part."

"Unless the Team gets into trouble or really needs us to protect their back," Doggie added and the three shook their heads in agreement.

"Very well," JJ confirmed, as he smiled at the three men knowing they, too, had developed a deep feeling for the Team.

CHAPTER TWO

It was a typical weekday morning rush hour at the Newark Train Station in downtown Newark, New Jersey. People filled the platforms waiting for Path Trains that arrived then departed with the destination of most passengers being New York City.

Amongst all of this commotion, the occasional Amtrak train would make a stop to take on commuters and other passengers bound for Penn Station in Manhattan.

Three men on the platform were neither commuters nor Amtrak travelers, they were Hezbollah terrorists and their travel plans ended in the middle of the Hudson River, as the train traveled through one of the tunnels that connected New Jersey to NYC.

They were traveling separately and pretended to be strangers to one another, but prior to arriving at the station, they had held their last meeting, went over the plan once again, and made sure the stopwatch part on their wristwatches were operating properly. Each man was carrying a briefcase filled with semtex high explosives and two detonators. To prevent a premature explosion, the detonators would not be armed until they were inside the tunnel. As the train entered the tunnel, each man would start his stopwatch, then arm the detonators, and wait for the proper time to detonate their bombs.

Other terrorist operatives had timed the ride several times and had calculated the approximate halfway point.

As the Amtrak train slowly pulled up then stopped, the crowd on the platform started to surge forward after conductors opened the doors on the train and allowed new passengers to board. Per their plan, the three would take a seat in separate cars and for maximum effect, detonate their explosives at the same time.

The three men acted as if they were not in any great hurry to board the train, as they stayed to the back of the crowd, but in reality, they were watching each other to make sure all would board the train.

Being the last or next to last persons to get on the train, they all found seats in separate cars, put the briefcases on their laps, and used them as desktops while pretending to review documents they had removed from their inside suit pockets. Nothing out of the ordinary, just businessmen preparing for a meeting in the city.

This was going to be a terrible wakeup call for the United States. With the main part of the war on terrorism being fought by clandestine forces, it did not show up in the media much and with the help of the liberals and left-wingers, the American People had yet again fallen asleep and would be awakened at another terrible cost.

As the train slowly moved away from the station, conductors started moving through the cars checking for tickets or railway passes. The two terrorists in the cars closer to the front of the train had no problems. They presented their tickets and the conductors moved onto the next person, but for the one toward the back of the train, it was a different story. He presented his ticket and as the conductor accepted it, he requested the briefcase be put on the floor. The terrorist should have complied, but instead, he objected and the conversation got heated. If it wasn't for the man sharing the seat with him calming things down and resolving the situation, it may have gotten out of hand.

After the conductor moved on, the man sharing the seat made a few disparaging comments about the conductor and the terrorist started to relax a little.

The train was now up to speed on the way to its next stop, but had not yet reached the tunnel entrance.

The plan for the explosions to occur in the middle of the tunnel was right out of the terrorist handbook. Create loss of life and/or destruction on a large scale to capture media attention for as long as possible. The bombs probably wouldn't create a breach in the tunnel itself, but the news that a passenger train exploded halfway between New Jersey and NYC along with all of the rescue efforts and the networks' terrorist experts giving their opinions, the disaster would dominate the media for a long time.

This attack may not have been a good idea. The 9/11 attack took the American people by complete surprise. The government took quick action in all areas and over the years since that day, things had sort of gotten back to normal.

Unlike the attack on Pearl Harbor when the country went to war until the enemy was defeated, this was a new, different kind of war, but Americans have a way of adjusting to things and the next time a big terrorist attack occurred on U.S. soil, the people would demand satisfaction in such a loud voice, the liberals and left-wingers would again go back into hiding under their rocks and the politicians would be forced to act as if they had the best interest of the United States at heart.

The train was getting close to the tunnel and the three terrorists were getting even more nervous. It was easy to say, *It will be for a great cause,* when one was talking about the deed, but after one realized in a matter of minutes that they would be in pieces, things were brought into clearer focus.

The terrorist seated toward the back of the train looked out the window to check the location, then reached down, grasped the handle of the briefcase, and lifted it onto his lap.

"Being a little risky aren't you?" a voice inquired and the terrorist quickly turned thinking he had been discovered, but instead saw the smiling face of the man sharing the seat.

"The conductor," the man explained to the terrorist.

"Oh, yeah," he nervously replied, then thought to himself, *In a short time, this stupid dog will not find things so amusing.*

A few minutes later, the train was entering the tunnel and all three men pushed buttons on their wristwatches starting their stopwatches, then pressed the latch releases on their briefcases and waited. It wouldn't be long before they all became martyrs in the eyes of Hezbollah and other terrorists around the world.

The seconds on the stopwatches clicked by moving closer and closer to detonation time. All three men watched intently and counted to themselves, then as if it were choreographed for a Broadway show, they all opened their briefcases just enough to reach inside and arm the detonators as they continued their counts to detonation and martyrdom.

Since this was the final destination for this Amtrak train, no one was on the platform to hear the announcement that came over the loudspeaker system. "Amtrak train number 640 is now arriving on track number 2. Thank you."

Amtrak train number 640 moved slowly along the platform, stopped, the conductors opened the doors, and all but three people moved quickly off the train to join the morning rush.

Three men with briefcases on their laps stayed in their seats and seemed to have drifted off to sleep. When the conductors approached each man to wake them, they all got a big surprise when they read a label that was stuck to the top of each briefcase. *Briefcase contains bomb. Call 9–1–1.*

As the conductors read, then reacted to the notes, seven men made their way through the pitch-black darkness of the tunnel behind the train on their way to one of the passageways used by the maintenance crews at the train station. Not wanting to use lights that might alert someone of their presence, the seven used only the two rails to guide them as they searched for the exit.

"Over here," a voice alerted.

As the seven men looked in the direction the voice seemed to have came from, they could see a dull green light and headed for it. When they got very close, they could make out a doorway and proceeded through it, first Benz followed by Panda, Check, Tic, Bris, Pru, and Met.

"We were wondering if you stopped for coffee along the way," Bean said to the seven.

"It's darker than a rat's ass out there," Panda replied.

"Everything go as planned?" Blue Jay inquired.

"Yes," Benz assured him.

"We almost had a moment when one of the terrorists got into a yelling match with the conductor, but Tic used his mediator skills and defused the situation before things got out of hand and we got blown to shit," Bris informed everyone.

"Good job," Blue Jay acknowledged. "Let's move out," he said, as he led the way.

All security cameras and other security devices along their exit route had been neutralized allowing the men to move quickly to ground level. Before exiting the passageways, Blue Jay and Bean distributed coveralls and hats worn by the real maintenance staff so they would blend in while exiting the building.

Leaving the passageway one at a time, the nine men found their way to one of three vehicles that were parked in the area. All would depart, then regroup a short time later, and change to other vehicles.

———————

That day at the Devil's Den, Di Flippi and Dunn had finally come to a compromise.

In the past, when the Team had neutralized terrorists on U.S. soil, the government had quickly covered it up so it wouldn't get out to the public.

Instead of letting the terrorists succeed with a terrible cost of innocent lives, they decided to employ the Team, let the results out in the open for all to see, and alert the media about the bombs on the train before the authorities could cover it up.

Just to make sure the train station wasn't put in lockdown before the media could get in any people, they got anonymous phone calls telling them about the bombs and even gave them the train number. By the time the police arrived, the media had already set up shop.

CHAPTER THREE

Night had fallen and the news about the three dead terrorists with bombs on an Amtrak train was burning up the airways.

All of the networks had their resident terrorist expert telling the public about where they thought the terrorists came from, how they were supplied, and some even guessed what color underpants the terrorists were wearing.

Two people knew exactly who supplied them and where they came from as they slowly crawled to another position for a better vantage point as they watched a house in a rural area of northern New Jersey.

Di Flippi not only had Intel about the train bombing, he also told Dunn about a QUD unit operating in New Jersey that would be supplying the bombers.

Additional intelligence gathering revealed when the plan to help bomb the train was first proposed, it caused a problem in Iran between the QUD leaders and a midlevel QUD officer who had an uncle with very high political connections.

The QUD ranking officers were against operations outside of the Middle East and especially in the U.S.

The uncle would not take no for an answer and had managed to convince the more powerful extremist side of the government to bypass the leaders of QUD, put his nephew in charge of a small group, and send them on the special mission to the United States.

One of the men in the darkness was very intent on watching the three men posted outside the house for security purposes when a voice whispered into his left ear, "You on?"

"I'm on," he whispered into the com unit he was wearing.

"Have your position and will join you," Blue Jay advised, as he started to crawl toward Jockey's location.

Arriving at Jockey's position, he inquired, "Where's JC?"

"Does the guard on the far left look familiar to you?" Jockey inquired, as he handed a night scope to Blue Jay.

As he looked through the scope, he muttered, "The man has no patience."

"Said he wanted a closer look," Jockey confirmed.

"And what a surprise I might add," Blue Jay replied.

Jockey then briefed him on the situation, total number of people, and the three, now two, men on guard duty.

While Jockey maintained surveillance, Blue Jay returned to brief the others. "We will break into two units. Benz, Panda, Check, Tic with Bean. Jockey, Bris, Pru and Met with me." With that done, he instructed the Team to move up.

When everyone was online with Jockey, Blue Jay, knowing JC was on the com, but unable to say anything, informed the others, "Everyone take note of that turd on the far left, he belongs to us. Unless he has decided to change sides and didn't tell anyone?"

The Team was wondering where JC was and smiled when they found out.

"Before going over the hill," Blue Jay continued, "JC performed recon on the entire area and told Jockey there were no windows or doors on the far side of the house thus eliminating any chance of escape on that side.

"We will advance along the same line toward the house with Bean's unit on the left covering mainly the front while the rest of us will be to the right covering the back. Any questions? No? Let's move out."

Blue Jay wasn't expecting any questions. After serving with this group for over seven years, he knew all he had to do was tell them about the situation and what was to be done. They already knew the how part.

To reduce the chance of detection, Blue Jay was the only one using night vision gear to keep track of the two men on guard outside of the house and that turd on the far left.

Two of the men outside were smoking up a storm, so between the smoke and the bright orange glow every time they took a puff on their cigarettes, it wasn't hard for the Team to keep track of their movements.

People smoking that much told the Team one of two things: The two men were either chain smokers or they were very nervous about the day's activities and were wondering if they had been compromised.

As the Team inched closer, a man came out of the house and after observing the two on guard, started yelling at them. The two immediately put out their smokes and stood at attention.

"He is reprimanding them and told them to start acting like soldiers," Check informed the others over the com units.

The man giving the reprimands then looked in the direction of the third guard standing in the dark a good distance away and as he shielded his eyes from the light coming out of the open door, yelled something.

"JC, just wave to him," Check said into the com and JC complied.

As the man headed back toward the house, Check informed everyone, "He told the men on security they were almost ready and would be moving to another location very soon."

"Let's pick up the pace," Blue Jay ordered.

The two guards had taken up better defensive positions and Blue Jay had informed the Team of their exact locations. One of the men took the reprimand to heart, but the other lit up another cigarette and waved his hand back and forth to disperse the smoke every time he exhaled.

After moving closer, Blue Jay halted the Team then instructed the two men closest to the security guards, "Check, Bris, on my mark." The two men quietly removed their 9mm Beretta pistols from their holsters, screwed on silencers, and started to crawl toward the men on security. The smoker was just thinking about smoking, but the younger man was more alert, so Bris had to take it very slow. When both men were in position, Blue Jay said, "Do it," and at almost the same second, two muffled sounds broke the silence and the two men were neutralized.

"Move out," Blue Jay instructed.

The Team stood up and moved toward the house. As they were about to cross the lawn that surrounded the house, a vehicle could be heard coming down the road that ran in front of the house. "Hold positions," came over the com. Everyone stopped and slowly went into a crouched position.

Blue Jay was on the com giving instructions in rapid fire. "If this vehicle pulls in here, we'll wait until they get out. Hopefully, someone will come out to greet them and before they realize their security men aren't responding, we'll hit them. If no one comes out, I'll give the word before they enter the house."

The Team was focused on the headlights of the vehicle as it came down the rural country road. At the speed it was traveling as it approached the driveway, it looked like it would pass by, but then it quickly slowed to make the turn. The Team members all looked down toward the ground so they would not give away their positions as headlight beams swung across the lawn and the wooded area. They quickly looked up again to watch as a van rolled to a stop in front of the house.

Two men got out of the front seat of the van and were heading toward the house. When it looked like no one would be coming out to greet them, Blue Jay said, "Let's do it," and the 10 men stood and quickly moved toward the house and van.

During some military assaults, gear can be heard rattling and banging as men run to assault a position, but not a sound could be heard as the Team proceeded across the lawn. Being dressed in black, they all blended into the night until the man in charge opened the front door and the light streaming out of the house exposed some of the group.

The man in the doorway saw the men and started to yell out the alarm, but JC quickly shut that down, then swung to his right, and downed one of the men from the van.

The Team didn't need any instructions on what to do at this point and took out the other man from the van. When the people inside realized what was happening, they grabbed their weapons and headed for the door, but two of them were put down before they got off a shot. The six remaining men saw they were in a bad situation, retreated to the back of the house, and out the kitchen door, but were intercepted by Blue Jay's group as they tried to flee across the side lawn.

A search of the house was conducted and no one else was found. Some documents that looked like they would be of interest to someone— explosives and detonators—were discovered and taken.

Satisfied that there was nothing more to be found at the house, JC ordered a withdraw.

As the Team departed via the front door, they saw Blue Jay standing on the front lawn deep in thought.

"Why don't I like this picture?" Bean inquired.

"Something wrong?" JC inquired.

"No, but I have an idea," Blue Jay answered.

"Told you I didn't like this picture," Bean reiterated.

"Didn't Mac tell us at the briefing the QUD leadership was having problems with a midlevel QUD officer and his uncle who had very heavy political power?" Blue Jay asked for confirmation.

"Yeah, so what's your point?" JC inquired.

"Well, we got the nephew, but the uncle is still around and is sure to cause more trouble especially when he finds out about his nephew. Sooo..." Blue Jay said with a smile.

———————

At four A.M., even the streets in New York City get pretty quiet.

It was particularly tranquil this morning until the noise from the engine of a van moving very slowly down the street broke the morning calm.

With one man behind the wheel and another in the passenger's seat, they seemed to be checking out the neighborhood or looking for a particular address. As it approached one of the very luxurious residences, it looked like the driver was more intent on looking than he was on driving as the van drifted toward the right, jumped the curb, and ran into one of the trees that lined the street.

After hitting the tree, the van just sat there. No effort to drive away or leave the scene on foot was made; it just sat there.

"Within a few minutes, sirens could be heard and vehicles flooded the area as both police and the media arrived at the scene.

Apparently, someone had called in a bomb scare saying the Iranian Ambassador to the United Nations was the intended target.

Once the area was secured, the bomb squad sent in a remote controlled robot equipped with a camera to get a look inside the van. When the robot reached the driver's side of the van, a powerful light mounted next to the camera was clicked on and the body of the robot was raised then moved close to the window. After viewing the front seat, the camera was swung to the right to check the rear on the van.

As the robot continued scanning the inside of the van, another police car came to a stop at the scene and a police captain got out. Seeing the new arrival, a lieutenant from the bomb squad walked over to report the situation.

"Find anything?" the captain inquired.

"Found what looks like explosives, a few detonators, and about thirteen dead bodies," the lieutenant reported.

In the shadows two blocks away, three men were observing the scene, then departed and got into a waiting vehicle around the corner.

"How do you think it will read in the press tomorrow?" Bean wondered aloud.

"If they print the info we supplied, it will say, *Iranian agents connected with the attempted train bombing showed up dead in front of their UN Ambassador residence,*" Blue Jay answered.

"You always have been mischievous, but what are you going to do if the Board strongly disapproves? JJ will be all over your ass," Bean advised.

"I'm just the backup Team Leader," Blue Jay replied with a smile.

"Just the backup Team Leader?" JC repeated. "Then I guess that makes me the one totally responsible?"

"That's about it," Blue Jay said then waited for the reply.

Total silence filled the vehicle and after a few seconds, the suspense made Blue Jay look at JC.

"Made you look didn't I, you peckerhead," and JC started a boisterous response everyone knew was coming.

———

The Board all agreed the van and the ambassador episode would enable the QUD leadership to get back control and keep activities out of the U.S. in the near future, but they were very unhappy about the Team doing something that major without prior approval from the Board.

Before the Team left on furlough, JJ had called a meeting to express the Board's strong disapproval. It turned out to be a pretty loud meeting with JJ reprimanding about not getting prior approval, JC and Blue Jay both trying to take the blame for the episode, and all of them yelling at the same time.

It seemed to be a dead heat until Panda yelled, "Do you mind if we leave?"

"Yeah, if you people are going to yell at each other, there isn't any reason for us to be here," Jockey added.

That put JJ over the top and after a pause, he yelled while throwing his hands into the air, "Yes, by all means get the hell out of here and take these two with you!"

The Team followed the instructions and JJ returned to the main house. As he opened the kitchen door, he was muttering, "Do you mind if we leave?" then shook his head.

"Did they get the word?" Mac inquired.

"For a second, I thought I got the message across, but only for a second," JJ replied with a smile.

CHAPTER FOUR

Per SOP's, the Team went on furlough after a Project's completion and were all due back within the next few days.

While the Team members were away, the House Team maintained security at the main house and the Barn in addition to their other duties.

Winter was still around with snow and ice storms making occasional visits.

On one cold afternoon, a stray kitten managed to find its way to the house and LadyA noticed it looking into the kitchen window as it sat on top of a stone wall that ran alongside the house.

Knowing the kitten must have been hungry, Top and the Ladies prepared food that would be suitable for a small kitten, but being on its own and afraid of people, the kitten ran away when they took out the food. Everyone knew if they just left the food on the deck that was outside of the kitchen and went back inside, the kitten would probably return for it.

To say the kitten was hungry would have been an understatement. While Top and the Ladies watched the kitten through the sliding glass door that led to the deck, the kitten watched them as it dove into the food. The slightest movement would bring the eating to a stop until it was sure no one was trying to get closer, and then the eating would continue.

It was close to dinnertime and first JJ, Mac, then the Team members that were back from furlough arrived and joined watching with the others. The kitten didn't care for all of the attention, but hunger kept the upper hand and it stayed until the food was all gone. When it had finished, the kitten licked its chops as it looked at all of the people then slowly turned and moved off keeping very low to the ground.

"I wonder where it came from?" LadyA said aloud.

"I wonder where it's staying," Lady1 inquired. "It's really too cold for a small kitten to be living outside on its own."

"Maybe we should do something about that," JJ suggested.

"It's probably too scared to come into the house," Top observed.

"Why don't we set up something out there?" Mac suggested.

Everyone thought that was a good idea. All offered to contribute to the effort and the following day, Project Kitty began.

Bris, Tic, and Check were putting together a temporary shelter. Starting with a cardboard box, they secured layers of newspaper pages to the outside for insulation and plastic garbage bags over the top of that to waterproof it. For the inside, they put more newspapers on the bottom and sides for additional insulation.

The trio were putting the finishing touches on the inside of the box when JJ arrived. "Anyone seen my Wall Street Journal?" he inquired.

"It may be part of the shelter," Bris answered.

"That's okay," JJ replied and left the room.

A few minutes later, JJ returned with carpet remnants from the last time he had new carpet installed in the house and an old sweat suit. "Maybe you can use these for the floor?" he said, handing the items to the men.

While the trio was telling JJ how they put the shelter together, General Mac was in the kitchen creating a toy until Jockey advised him that his idea sucked and after the usual verbal skirmish between the two, they started working on the toy together.

A heavy sweat sock was balled up and there was twine wrapped tightly around it leaving a two-foot length of the twine. While Jockey added a rubber band to the end of the twine, then more twine, Mac used another sweat sock to cover the balled up one then tied twine around it.

Pleased with their creation, Mac and Jockey were testing it when JJ appeared in the doorway. "Another creation?" he observed with a smile.

"We're thinking about marketing it," Mac announced then added, "We'll call it, The Wilson," he declared.

Not knowing their real names, Jockey was unaware that Mac was referring to Charley Wilson, one of the Board members he had frequent humorous jousting matches with.

JJ just smiled as he observed how the rubber band would cause the sock to pull back each time the kitten pulled on it.

Benz, Panda, Pru, and Met took the easy way out, made an early morning trip to PetMart, and returned with a scratching post complete with bell and a round bed.

Top and the Ladies took on the responsibility of feeding it and had already purchased a supply of 9 Lives canned and dry food and snacks for the kitten.

Later in the day, the kitten was spotted in the area. Food, along with all of the other items, were put out on the deck and everyone watched as the kitten cautiously approached the deck, again keeping very low to the ground and noticing everything that moved or made a sound. Once it got to the edge of the deck, it quickly looked over the edge, and then ducked down.

"You could learn a few things from this kitten's tactics," Panda informed Jockey.

"I'd say something, but I don't want to scare it away," he replied and both men smiled.

Knowing the food was there, but not sure about the other new items, it very cautiously inspected each item on its way to the food, and then settled in for some chow as everyone watched the kitten and it watched all of them.

JC was the last to arrive and displayed the toy he had created. One end of a long piece of twine ran through the middle of a tennis ball and was secured. Halfway up the length of twine, a rubber band was inserted followed by additional twine. "Cats like these types of things especially if you tie it to a line of some sort," JC announced.

"Can I see that?" Mac asked. JC handed it to him.

"Let me see," Mac said, as he inspected the toy. "Twine with a rubber band inserted in the middle. A tennis ball with the name Wilson printed on it. Where have I seen something like this before?" Mac pretended to wonder, as he looked at his toy tied to the patio table outside. Mac then bent down still looking out the window and said, "Kitty, I think we have a copycat in here."

"Give me a break," JC spoke up, "everybody knows about using a rubber band and all I could find around here was a Wilson tennis ball."

"I don't know, sounds pretty dubious to me," Mac observed.

"He was probably snooping in the kitchen window when we were making ours," Jockey added.

"Yeah, that's what I did," JC replied. "No offense, Kitty, but the man that learned how to fly at Pussy Airways has found me out."

The conversation started to get a little loud, but since everyone was laughing, the kitten figured it couldn't be too serious and kept on eating as it watched the activities inside.

The following morning, Blue Jay, then Bean returned from furlough. The Team was all at breakfast, so they went to the main house to join them. After breakfast, they were told about the kitten and how everyone had contributed.

"That's nice," Bean approved.

"We do need one thing and we all thought that maybe you two could get it," LadyA announced.

"Sure, what is it?" Blue Jay asked.

"A litter box," she replied.

"And kitty litter," Lady1 added.

Blue Jay looked at Bean and said, "Another shit detail."

"I think a Dear Ma letter is in order," Bean replied, as the duo turned, headed for the door, and sang aloud, "Dear Ma, Fucked again. Love, your son."

"And don't forget the scoops and stuff," LadyA yelled, as the other Team members yelled out directions to PetMart

A few minutes had passed when the duo returned.

"Does this kitten have a name?" Blue Jay inquired.

"We were thinking about getting a monogrammed shit pot," Bean explained.

"No, but I guess the kitten should have one," Lady1 replied and everyone started thinking.

"I get a kick out of the way it peeks over the edge of the deck then ducks down at chow time," Panda offered.

"Sometimes it looks like it's playing peek-a-boo," LadyA added.

"How about Peeka?" Top offered.

"That works," Panda said and everyone agreed.

"Well, where is Peeka?" the duo inquired and everyone left the table to see if the kitten was in the area.

———————

Several weeks had passed, Peeka was starting to trust the people in the new home and was even using the new monogrammed litter box.

One day, everyone was concerned because Peeka, instead of running around and playing with the toys, was just lying around and looking very uncomfortable.

It was around dinnertime, some of the Team members were arriving and they were almost knocked over backward by the odor when they opened the kitchen door.

Never wasting an opportunity, Jockey said in a loud voice, "Another one of Top's specialties no doubt. It's obvious he was not paying attention when he got this recipe from *Emeril Live.*"

"He probably fell asleep during the show and woke up in the middle of *Farmer's Weekly.* The pig shit can be useful edition," Panda added.

"Hand me that big spoon," Top said, as he continued preparing the evening meal.

"Not again," Jockey told him, as he quickly moved past to see what was really causing the smell.

"Well, I guess we know what the problem was," Lady1 said, as she watched Peeka run around the area.

"What the hell," JJ commented, as he entered the kitchen. "Mac, quick, close the door to the dining room."

The shit pot duo was elected and under the supervision of LadyA, was attempting to get rid of the relic in the litter box that was causing the odor.

While Blue Jay held a plastic bag, Bean used a scoop to troll for the goodie.

"You're not doing it right," LadyA instructed while holding her nose.

"Not doing it right? I can't even breathe," Bean informed her, as he gasped for air.

"Is that it?" Blue Jay pointed.

"I don't think anything that small can smell that bad," Bean said, but retrieved it anyway and bagged it.

After every downstairs door and window were opened, the smell started to subside.

As everyone passed through the kitchen on their way to the dining room, Jockey said in a loud voice, "Remind me to never eat any of Top's leftovers," and was immediately hit on the head by something.

As Jockey looked in the direction of where it came from, Top said, "Got the big spoon myself," as he shook it in his direction.

"Will the lad ever learn?" Mac inquired as the Team continued to laugh, as they made their way down the hall to the dining room.

CHAPTER FIVE

Big Face with all of his money and runaway ego thought he was the king of South America and in 2006, when the Team took out an Al-Qaida training camp in Chile, in his mind, it was an invasion into his monarchy.

He wanted to know who was responsible so he could hold them accountable, but had been unsuccessful in identifying who they were.

In 2007, when the Team foiled his plans to control Cuba from behind the scenes and assuming it was the same group that invaded Chile, he pulled out all the stops to find out who was responsible.

Almost a year had passed and Big Face was still trying to find out their identity. He held weekly meetings to get a status report, though usually to no avail.

The meeting being held during the first week of January 2008 would have ended the same way if one of his inner circle of advisors hadn't asked to express an idea.

Being granted permission, the advisor stated, "Maybe we have been going about this in the wrong direction. The fact that whoever it was had knowledge about the training camp in Chile, one had to wonder at that time, if the information came from rumors that tend to circulate about such things or from an intelligence source."

"After our plans for Cuba were foiled and if it was the same group, it is obvious a connection to some intelligence service in the U.S., South America, or both is real."

"The fact they have maintained a very low profile and have been impossible to identify indicates a military, intelligence, or a high end contract group, but whoever they are, my guess is the U.S. is behind it." All agreed.

"To date, we have been trying to find out who these people are by searching for information or anything that would give us a clue about their identity, but we have been unsuccessful." He continued. "Instead of trying to seek them out, why don't we change strategy, try to bring them to us and crush them once and for all."

Big Face liked what he was hearing and added, "If we could take some prisoners, I can parade them in front of the media saying U.S. death squads are assassinating the people of South America. If they aren't Americans, I can do the same thing, but say all of the assassins have been killed."

"Do you have any ideas about how we could lure them into a trap? If they are professionals, it will not be an easy task," another top advisors inquired.

"It would all depend on how much of a risk we would be willing to take," the advisor replied. "We are allowing tons of cocaine to be distributed to the U.S. and Europe each year, the Iran arms deals to Central and South America we broker, and diamond smuggling. We could somehow make one of them a desirable target."

"We are making too much money in those areas to run the risk of losing or bring unwanted attention to them," Big Face ruled. "Do you have anything else?"

"I have one idea that may be too enticing for whoever is controlling this group to turn down, but it could also backfire on us if it became known outside of our country."

"What is it?" Big Face eagerly inquired. The advisor explained his idea.

———————

Another small Project had been completed, the Team's furlough time was coming to an end, and all were preparing to return to home base and the Barn.

This time for his furlough, Blue Jay had decided to go someplace warm and was enjoying the sun, sea, and beach at Lime Tree Villas in Ocho Rios, Jamaica. Since his flight was scheduled to leave in two days, he decided to enjoy some of the local nightlife before returning to New Jersey.

Jamaica was a good place for anyone to relax and unwind from their day job and this was especially true for someone in Blue Jay's line of work.

Having made the rounds to most of the four and five star hotels along the beach, he decided it was time for some shuteye and headed back to the villa he had rented for the month.

After being in Jamaica for that length of time, Blue Jay was totally unwound and maybe a little less cautious as he unlocked, then opened the front door of the villa. He was still thinking about some of the enjoyable night activities as he closed the door and flipped on the switch that lit up the room, but got a rude awakening as he looked up.

"Just keep walking," the man sitting in a chair facing the door instructed, as he pointed a silenced automatic pistol at Blue Jay's chest.

Blue Jay was surprised to see the man, but recovered quickly as the man inquired, "Surprised to see me?"

"Yeah," he replied. "I thought you would still be in the front window at Home Depot."

"That's just another reason to kill you. Take off your jacket, drop it to the floor, and slowly turn around. Remember, I am very quick and a deadly shot."

"Oh, I remember," he assured the man and complied with his instructions.

Having made the turn, he was instructed to sit on the couch that put him in a direct line with the man in the chair.

"I first saw you by accident and figured you were down here after me, but after watching your activities, I knew that was not the case," the man explained. "I was going to depart for Kingston, but since I'm low on cash and have a feeling you are privy to certain information worth a lot of money to certain people, figured I would stick around.

"I have been following you for the past several days, but not too much. You know how it works, just when I figured you were getting that feeling someone was following; I would break off. Kept that routine up until you led me to this place."

"You must be slipping. I could have easily killed you, but first, I wanted to have a little chat."

"Funny, I was just thinking the same thing about you," Blue Jay replied. "About the slipping part I mean."

"I can still deal with the likes of you," the man's ego made him blurt out.

"Then why did you bring help?"

"What?" the man said, as he took a quick glance at the sliding glass door that led to a patio. "Don't even try that shit with me," the man advised, regaining his composure.

"No?" Blue Jay questioned. "Well, there's somebody out there. Question is which one of us are they after?"

"Keep it up and I'll put a hole in you right now."

"Okay, okay, my mistake. I just thought they came with you," Blue Jay gave in. "You said something about having a chat?" he asked.

"More like getting information," he replied. "After you caused me to wreck that Corvette in Jersey two years, those troopers got to the scene before I could get away. They took me into custody and it took me eighteen months before I could escape from prison. Now I need money, a lot of money, and you are going to help me solve that problem."

"What information could I have that would be worth that much money?"

"Information about a group that have been selectively taking out terrorist activities around the world. I'm sure people with a lot of money to spare are trying to identify that group and I figure I could sell the information to the highest bidder and make a very large sum of money in the process," he replied. "Now, I could start putting holes in you, but that may make you hard to understand or cause you to pass out, so we'll try it the easy way first."

Already knowing this fucker was crazy, Blue Jay figured he better play along, so after a little pretending that he didn't know anything, he started telling his story. Not knowing how much Crazy already knew, he carefully mixed a little truth with a lot of fiction.

He wasn't interrupted while telling his tale and when he had finished, Crazy said, "You gave me a lot of useful information, if I was writing a fairytale. Now knock off the shit and give me the real info," Crazy insisted, threatening with the gun.

"You didn't expect the straight stuff on the first try did you?" Blue Jay inquired, suggesting the truth would be forthcoming. "All of this talking has made my throat dry. Mind if I get a drink?"

"Normally, I would say no," Crazy answered, "but you almost have me to the point where I don't care about the money and just want to kill you, so get your drink and I hope you try something."

Blue Jay knew Crazy wasn't kidding, as he moved to a small bar where he had the makings for his favorite drink. "Mind if I get ice?" he asked for permission.

"No," Crazy replied, getting very anxious and hoping Blue Jay would give him a reason to kill him on the spot.

Knowing this, Blue Jay just went about making his lime martini. First cracked ice into a martini shaker, Ketel One vodka, and Rose's Lime Juice. "I suppose you wouldn't let me cut up a fresh lime would you?" he asked.

"Do what you want," Crazy approved, knowing with a knife in his hand, he may be tempted to try something.

Blue Jay started to reach for the knife and Crazy tightened his grip on the silenced .22 automatic, but halfway through reaching for the knife he stopped, thought about it, then changed his mind.

"Just lime juice is good enough," he said aloud, as he put the top onto the new Ketel One martini shaker he had brought on vacation with him. "Am I taking too long?" he inquired.

"As a matter of fact you are," Crazy answered in a voice that was starting to lose patience.

Blue Jay quickly started shaking the container until the top got frosty, then removed a smaller top on the shaker so he could pour the beverage through the built-in strainer and into a martini glass. Halfway through the pour, he stopped and looked at the sliding glass door to the patio.

"Now what?" Crazy inquired.

"Nothing," he replied. He completed the pour, put the little top back onto the shaker, and quickly returned to his seat.

After taking a sip of the drink, he declared, "That's good stuff," then started to take a second sip. The second sip was longer and it seemed he was savoring it.

Crazy was very intent on watching Blue Jay's every move when a sound much like the noise of a super silenced weapon being fired was heard in the area of the patio doors. Without hesitation, Crazy quickly turned and fired in the direction of the noise, drilled the martini shaker dead center, and it went flying up against the wall.

Blue Jay was hoping that noise would occur when enough pressure built up inside the new shaker to pop off the small cap on the top of the shaker. It had gotten his attention more than once during his stay and for the same reason.

First, he tossed his glass in the direction of Crazy's head as he moved to the right.

Knowing Blue Jay would take advantage of the situation, Crazy quickly returned his attention back to him. After sweeping aside a glass that was coming straight at his face, he fired two rounds in the direction where Blue Jay was sitting.

He was quick and deadly, but he wasn't Superman and the distractions gave Blue Jay all of the time he needed to close the distance between himself and Crazy.

Realizing he had just pumped two rounds into the couch, he quickly looked to his left and saw the end of a wicker coffee table rapidly approaching. As with the glass, he tried to sweep it aside and fire his weapon, but with Blue Jay's full weight behind the table as he charged, it didn't work out. The table made full contact with his upper torso, the force of the impact sent his chair over backward and a round was fired into the ceiling.

Blue Jay was bending forward, but managed to maintain his footing as he, Crazy, and the coffee table rode the chair over backward. With the weapon being his primary concern, he kicked the hand holding the pistol with his right foot. As the weapon went sliding across the floor, Crazy reached up and grabbed Blue Jay's shirt with his left hand and forcefully planted his right foot into his lower abdomen, then pulled down sharply with his arm and pushed up very hard with his leg. Not being allowed to fully recover after he kicked the gun loose, Blue Jay was a little off-balance and Crazy managed to pull him across his body then toss him into the air and against the wall to their left.

Having a foot jammed into his abdomen then being slammed against a wall, Blue Jay's insides seemed to be rolling around, but there was no time to think about that now as he scrambled to his feet.

Crazy had done a backward roll to get clear of the chair, came up on his feet, and was already attacking with a right kick to the solar plexus.

Blue Jay quickly stepped back and using his right arm, performed a downward sweeping block, and then managed to hook the heel of the attacking foot with his right hand turning the attacker into the defender.

Being in perfect position to deliver a side kick to the groin area and knowing that was the obvious attack, Blue Jay started to perform a right side thrust kick, but halfway through its execution, stopped, and executed a hopping-type movement, as he dropped his right foot to the floor, lifted his left foot up, and delivered a crescent kick to the right side of the rib cage. He followed up with a powerful punch that landed between his eyes that ended the confrontation and Crazy's dark career.

CHAPTER SIX

The other Team members had already returned from furlough when Blue Jay walked into the Barn.

Everyone was either working out with the weights, was on a treadmill, or on the large matted area in the middle of the big open space practicing Judo, karate, or other martial arts with Benz and Panda.

As Blue Jay walked in, he greeted everyone as he headed for the stairs that led to the second floor and the rooms assigned to the Team members.

Bean noticed Blue Jay seemed a little uptight and inquired, "Everything all right?"

"Yes and no. Let me stow this gear then I'll fill you in," he replied, as he continued up the stairs.

It was getting close to dinnertime and everyone decided to get ready and go over to the house early to see what Peeka had been up to.

Spring had finally made its appearance and Peeka had finally made friends with everyone. Coming into the house and Barn, but was still primarily an outside cat with the deck being the main hangout. Being young and frisky, Peeka would play with the toys and even turned the round bed into a toy by lying down alongside it and spinning it like a top. Natural instincts were also developing. First stalking insects then birds came into play.

One day, House and Barn activities had come to a standstill when Peeka was seen stalking a very young deer in the field behind the Barn, as the mother deer continued to graze close by keeping an eye on the activity. Being an orphan, no one was around to teach Peeka things like what was too big to stalk, but it probably wouldn't have mattered anyway. A few days later, a group of six deer filed across the property and were immediately stalked as they crossed the field and into the woods beyond.

The question about gender was an ongoing wonderment and one day, Mac thought he had a clue when Peeka was laying down batting and grabbing the Wilson sock toy.

"I see ninnies," Mac had sung out, notifying everyone that Peeka might be a female.

"General Mac!" Lady1 scolded, as she quickly stood up straight and pushed against the top of her blouse.

"What? Oh! I meant Peeka," Mac defended, until he noticed everyone was laughing and realized she was joking.

When Peeka took little trips and was gone for a while, everyone inquired about her and if she were not back within a day or so, they would get a little concerned.

JJ did overhear a story in the barber shop told by a man that lives down the road from the Barn, but there is no way of knowing if the cat was Peeka.

He said, "Sometimes when looking out of the window I will see my cat Randall running across the lawn with a smaller cat close behind batting at his tail. What makes it funny, Randall is a tom cat about four times the size of the smaller cat, but he allows the cat to chase him. He will fight other cats in a second, but I guess he just likes the little cat?"

Where Peeka goes was the topic of conversation when Blue Jay entered the room and after listening for a while, he inquired, "Any of you assholes ever think about following her to see where she goes?"

Silence filled the room for about three seconds, then all hell broke loose and things finally quieted down when it was decided Blue Jay, AKA The Great White Hunter, would track Peeka the next time she headed out. When Peeka left for one of her trips, she always seemed to follow the same route of departure. Up the lane, past the Barn, into the field next to the Barn, then headed toward the woods beyond. After that, it was anybody's guess, but The Great White Hunter would be sure to solve that mystery the next time out.

The following morning, Blue Jay requested a meeting with JJ, Mac, the Team, and House Team to inform them about his encounter in Jamaica and about whether he should leave the Team in case Crazy had told someone about his suspicions. He was reasonably sure Crazy was not lying about the chance encounter, but with him, you could never be sure. He may have been sent by someone or even started marketing the information before he had possession of it and that could spell trouble.

After the meeting had gone on for a few hours, it was decided that Blue Jay would not leave the Team. The Team members would sniff around to see if any rumors were circulating about information being offered up to the highest bidder about a secret group that was attacking the terrorist network.

JJ and Mac briefed the Board the following morning who also discussed it to great lengths before coming to the same conclusion as the Teams and would also sniff around. Foxie, with his extensive contacts with Nav Intel and other military intelligence types, Dawson with his Oil Intel Group, and Dunn would check in with Di Flippi and other sources.

The Board and Teams concluded that Crazy was playing a lone hand and since he was no longer around to continue his efforts, there would no longer be a threat, but it was always better to be sure than be sorry, so preventative measures would be taken and everyone would stay more alert to daily occurrences.

Several days had passed since the challenge was issued to the Great White Hunter and the Team was all at the Barn when one of the phones rang. Bean answered it, said a few words, and then hung up. "Word has it Peeka may be heading out on a trip," he said loudly.

A few seconds later, Blue Jay was quickly moving down the stairs and heading toward the front door to try to catch a glimpse of the black and white critter as she passed the Barn.

"Isn't Peeka going to have an advantage in the dark?" Panda inquired.

"Not if I'm wearing these," Blue Jay explained, as he held up a pair of night vision goggles.

"Is The Great White Hunter cheating?" Jockey inquired.

"I think we should call the rules committee about this," Panda added and the Team chimed in.

Bean was in the forefront of the assault when JC appeared on the scene. "Bean, can I have your assistance with a technical problem?"

"Sure," Bean agreed and the two retreated toward the room where JC had all of the neat technical gizmo stuff squirreled away.

The Great White Hunter ignored all of the harassment as he scanned the area in front of the Barn. He thought he had missed her, but at the last second, caught a glimpse of what looked like the white on Peeka's right hind leg slowly taking a step as she entered the edge of the field.

"There you are," Blue Jay said to himself, as he moved to the end of the Barn and entered the field via a side door. After putting on his night vision gear, he could see Peeka making her way across the field. He knew a cat's night vision was very good, but he wasn't sure how good, so he kept a good distance until they got close to the wooded area when he closed the gap, that way he could keep sight of her in the woods.

She doesn't seem to be in any hurry. Just following this deer trail to her destination, he thought, as he moved slowly through the woods.

One second she was there, and then she was gone.

How in the hell did she disappear so quickly? he wondered.

I bet she lived out here before coming to the house. Maybe in a hole or something, he reasoned, as he moved closer. When he got to the spot where she disappeared, he got down on hands and knees so he wouldn't scare Peeka and cause her to run. *Let me see, had sight of her until she passed this big oak, so she must be close,* he reasoned and started scanning from his left side and moving to the right. All of the sudden, he heard what sounded like a large animal charging through the plant life and heading in his direction. He quickly turned his head and looked back to his left just in time to see what at first glance looked like a mountain lion up on its hind legs and batting at the green glow the night vision goggles were giving off.

"You almost gave me a fuckin' heart attack!" a startled Blue Jay yelled, then gave out a hearty laugh.

Peeka, thinking this was a neat game, ran off to hide again in the bushes.

"No, I ain't playing anymore," Blue Jay declared, as he stood up and started walking back toward the Barn still laughing.

After walking a short distance, he noticed someone had joined him. Peeka was also heading back to the Barn and had decided to keep him company.

"You led me right into that one," he said.

Peeka responded with a very long meow that sort of went up and down as it went along.

"You are a talker, cat, aren't you?" Blue Jay said with surprise and additional laughter.

She again responded, but not as long.

This conversation lasted for the remainder of the walk back and covered things like, *I'll give you a treat if you keep this our little secret.*

Blue Jay was really getting a kick out of this. He had relaxed and was his old self again.

When they entered the Barn, the Team, House Team, even JJ and Mac had gathered around the entertainment center.

"Join us," Lady1 invited. "When you were all on furlough, we started a movie night."

Being in a better mood than when he first got back from furlough, he agreed and sat down next to Lady1 as JC popped a video cassette into the VCR.

The opening scene had been shot at night and showed a man on hands and knees by a giant oak tree.

Blue Jay started laughing. "This is the second time I've been had tonight."

"Wait a minute, here comes the best part," Lady1 informed him as she nudged him with her elbow.

JC and Bean didn't have to get close at all to get both video and audio of both The Great White Hunter tracking and the walk back from the woods.

The video gave everyone, including Blue Jay, a good laugh and it was viewed more than once.

After the third viewing, LadyA leaned down and inquired, "Did you scare Uncle Blue Jay in the woods?" She was answered with a short, "Meow," followed by a very long one.

"No kidding," Mac acknowledged.

"What did she say, Mac?" Panda inquired.

"She said all of the excitement has given her an appetite."

"I could go for something to eat myself," Jockey added and the others agreed.

"Come on," Top said, pretending to be annoyed, but really wasn't, as he stood up and walked toward the door.

Knowing Top was probably going back to where the goodies were kept, Peeka quickly walked alongside him. "See what you started?" Top inquired and another conversation began.

CHAPTER SEVEN

The Board was again in session and in the process of selecting the next Project. If a Board member had a Project in mind, they would present it to the others. After each presentation, the Board would discuss it. If need be, the Projects were narrowed down to three, then voted on.

The Board usually didn't have a problem when selecting their next Project, but this time, they were divided across the three and JJ had to schedule this special session to continue the process.

They had discussed and voted on the Projects all afternoon, but the count was still 3, 3, 1.

After the last vote was taken, JJ took the floor. "Well, gentlemen, this is a new one for us. To date, we have always managed to agree on a Project and never had to address a situation like this, but there is a first time for everything." He continued. "I guess it's time to start the process from the beginning."

"I probably have the tie breaker, but I hesitate to present it," Dunn spoke up.

"I was thinking more along the lines of starting over with three new Projects, but if the other Board members don't mind you presenting a new one…" JJ questioned and the members all agreed.

"The reason I am hesitant is due to a feeling I have more than anything else," Dunn confessed. "It is a very desirable Project, within our capabilities, and just right for the Team to execute. In fact, it may be just a little too right."

"Have a feeling someone may be laying a trap?" General Mac inquired, as he moved closer to the table.

"Could be," Dunn admitted. "We have been active all over the world including Central and South America and the location of this Project would be the ideal place for a trap."

"Do you think they know about the Team?" Howard asked.

"It's probably a fishing expedition if anything at all, but since Blue Jay's encounter in Jamaica, I can't be totally sure," Dunn replied.

"Why don't you go ahead and present it, so we all can get the entire picture?" JJ suggested.

With that, Gil stood and walked to the easel in front of the room and started. "The Project location would be on the Island of Tottuga off the coast of South America." He paused knowing there would probably be comments.

"Big Face again," Wilson said aloud. "He should be one of our Projects."

"I'm working on it," JJ assured him.

After waiting a short time, Dunn continued. "You all may have seen in the media about an Al-Qaida training camp being discovered on the Afghanistan—Pakistan border. What made it a unique find was the fact that all trainees looked like American and European types thus enabling them to move around more easily in western countries. Since the camp was discovered, it had to be relocated and what better place than under Uncle Sam's nose where they could go undetected and enter the U.S. by land or sea." "We have been unable to find out who made first contact. If it was Al-Qaida, it could just be a smart move. If it was Big Face, it could be part of an elaborate scheme to entice those people responsible for ruining his plans for Cuba."

"And we are sure this camp is there and not just a deception?" JJ inquired.

"Ho, it's there all right and operational," Dunn confirmed, then continued with the exact location and other details.

When Gil had finished, Foxie was the first to ask a question. "I'm sure the U.S. Government knows about this, so what is their reason for not acting this time?"

"The politicians in Washington are afraid if military action is taken, the U.S. would look like an aggressor in South America and if clandestine action was taken and failed, it would have the same result as taking military action," Dunn explained.

"Same old, same old," Foxie commented.

"Are there any other avenues we could explore to give us a better picture of the situation and who made first contact?" Mac inquired.

"Swabbie has a contact that used to be in the intelligence business and maintained contacts after he left the service. If you want to proceed on a fact finding basis only, we could make inquiries," Gil suggested.

After additional discussion, the Board decided they did want more facts and would include the Team in the fact finding.

They also decided the Project wasn't serious enough to expose the Team to any unnecessary risk and if anything even remotely pointed to a possible trap, it would be voted down.

CHAPTER EIGHT

When JJ formed the group, it was decided for security reasons the Board and Team would not be privy to the identity or ever see the other. Codenames were assigned to each Team member and were used instead of their real names. The rule stayed in effect until one of the Projects caused the Team and Board to interact and in the process, they all became fast friends. After that, the rule was eased and everyone attended the occasional dinner party held at the Barn, but that was the extent of their meetings.

It was decided in this case, instead of JJ and Mac relaying the information and maybe not being able to answer certain questions, Dunn himself would give the briefing and as in the past, the Team would set up security and supply transportation to and from the Barn.

Since Gil had been an intelligence operative in the past, even if someone was trying to follow him, they would have been hard-pressed and after he made contact with the Team, it would have been impossible for any person or persons to maintain surveillance without being spotted by a Team member.

First Benz and Panda arrived at the Barn followed shortly by Gil and JC. All got out of their cars, went into the Barn, and proceeded to the Team meeting room to wait for the others to return. Top and the Ladies had refreshments on hand and greeted Gil. "Good to see you again, Mr. Black," Top addressed him by his assigned codename. "Would you like some coffee?"

"Sounds good," Dunn answered, as he rubbed his hands together. Spring had officially arrived, but it was still a little nippy at night.

After Dunn got his coffee, he chatted with everyone for a while then walked to the front of the room where he would give the briefing.

Swabbie, Jar Head, and Doggie entered the room, joined him, and after the usual greetings, Gil inquired, "Where are your adopted children?" He was addressing the question to Jar Head and Doggie.

"Ho, they'll be along I suppose, if they don't decide to give chase to a terrorist or something," Doggie replied.

"Yeah, they'll be here soon, and then we can all reminisce about the old days at the Agency when we used to drive the DDO bullshit. Now what was his name?" Jar Head pretended not to remember it was Gil.

"Things haven't changed much have they?" Dunn observed.

"Did you think they ever would?" Swabbie asked.

"No!" Dunn answered quickly and all four burst into laughter.

The remainder of the Team had arrived with Blue Jay and Bean being the last to enter the room.

The four men were still at the front of the room having a serious conversation. They didn't see the duo arrive and a short time later, they heard a voice saying, "Looks like something serious," Blue Jay observed.

"Nah, they're probably just telling him about Fort Old Farts," Bean offered.

Gil didn't know anything about Fort Old Farts, but was sure he would know all about it before he left.

"I guess we can get started," JJ said in a loud voice and everyone took a seat.

"Good to see you all again. The Board sends their best and looks forward to seeing you at the next dinner party here at the Barn," Gil relayed, then after a pause, started with the briefing.

"I am here because the Board is considering a new Project, but for this one, we feel the need to change the SOPs. As in the past, we have done our homework, discussed the Project, but due to someone on the Board having a bad feeling about it," Dunn said, as he raised his hand indicating it was him, "the Board would like additional Intel gathered before voting on it and requests you all to join in the gathering of information.

"As in the past, if the Board approves the Project, it will be sent onto you for consideration."

Gil then covered the Project itself including the reasons for his concern. After presenting all of the information, Gil said,

"Now that everyone is up to date, I'll cover what we are doing to get a better picture. Board members are getting in touch with sources they have and through general conversation are bringing up the training camp and why the government isn't doing anything. After they get their contacts on the topic, they will try to extract additional information about who called whom first. We would appreciate it if you people would make very discreet contacts and try to find how information about the training got out in the first place.

"Our original source said their information came out of Columbia. Being in the general area news about the camp could have just traveled to Columbia and made its way to the grapevine, but it could have also been planted knowing it would eventually be discovered by whoever is attacking the terrorist network. Any questions?" Dunn inquired and of course there were.

The Team didn't have any problems about doing extra Intel, especially since Mr. Black had a bad feeling about the Project. Sometimes feelings and instincts can keep you alive when you are involved in clandestine activities.

When all of the questions and concerns were addressed, Dunn adjourned the meeting by saying, "Top and the Ladies have additional refreshments waiting at the house. I'll join you there after I get the scoop on Fort Old Farts." Everyone laughed, as they stood up then filed out of the meeting room.

Finding out the scoop about Fort Old Farts was not a lie, but Gil also wanted to talk with Swabbie, Jar Head, and Doggie about their contact in the Caribbean who used to be a Cuban intelligence officer. Everyone at the meeting could be completely trusted, but Dunn was from the old school where on-a-need-to-know basis was one of the golden rules and he didn't want to discuss the matter in an open meeting.

While the others were leaving the room, Gil was brought up to date about the Fort Old Farts. Having worked with and for Dunn in the past, Swabbie knew there was more to this than wanting to hear about the Fort.

With the story completed and only Swabbie, Jar Head, and Doggie remaining in the room, Dunn said, "You probably already know what I'm going to say don't you?" Dunn said, looking at the three men.

"Our source in the Caribbean," Swabbie spoke up.

"Yes, and I was wondering how you feel about contacting him?" he inquired.

"We haven't been in touch for a while and he moves from time to time to keep his family safe ever since he got discussed and left Cuba."

"I wouldn't want to put him or his family into any unnecessary danger, so I'll leave that call up to you," Dunn replied.

"I think we are all in agreement that our source taking an active role and going back into the field is too dangerous and totally unacceptable," Swabbie said. He paused to make sure Jar Head and Doggie agreed. "But he does seem to have good sources that keep him in the know about intelligence matters in Central and South America, so we could make arrangements to meet with him."

"Whatever you think is best," Gil agreed.

"For his safety, it would be a very brief meeting in a place of his choosing. Doggie and Jar Head will not attend the meeting, but will act as security and I am sure the two sons of our source will also be in the area. I will send one text message to him that looks like a vanilla question, but includes words that will ask for a meeting and give him the area we would like information about. He will in turn send a vanilla message back to me."

"Aren't you concerned about your coded messages getting intercepted and decoded?" Dunn inquired.

"If anyone decodes it, they may be wrong," Swabbie replied with a smile. "There are only two words in the entire message the source will consider. One tells him we want info and the other identifies the area we are concerned about. If he replies with an answer to the question, it will include the location, a date, and we will meet five days before that date. If he doesn't answer the question, his reply is no. We'll create the message and send it off tomorrow morning," Swabbie concluded.

Thinking their business was completed, Dunn turned and started to leave to join the others at the house when Jar Head said, "There is one other thing. We have a video we would like you to see before you go to the house."

Dunn was a little puzzled, but figured it might be something concerning the Board or Team in the area of security or something worse, so he rejoined the three men.

———

Some time had passed when Gil, Swabbie, Jar Head, and Doggie finally joined the others at the house. When they walked in, Peeka walked over to take a look at the man she had never seen before.

Gil bent down and put the back of his hand toward her, so she could check out his scent and at the same time said in a loud voice, "Blue Jay, when I heard you were chasing pussy, this was not the first thing that came to mind. I thought we might have a possible security problem, but your agency fathers have straightened everything out."

Blue Jay was caught totally off-guard and didn't know who to counterattack first, Gil or the other three, then decided on Dunn since he would be leaving soon.

"Well, guess I won't be able to use my fish material for obvious reasons, but I'll think of something," Blue Jay said, as he started his coun-terattack.

The three men with Dunn started to laugh knowing he was referring to the very first time the two met and Dunn, wanting to see how the new young man would react, said in a mocking man-ner, "Blue Jay! Isn't that just a pretty bird?" He answered in the same mocking manner. "Gil! isn't that part of a fish?" Not usually the type of thing one says when meeting the DDO at CIA.

Dunn and Blue Jay were off to the races as everyone sat back and had a lot of laughs. The two were very careful not to give away anything they shouldn't, but both still had a lot of material about things that happened during their time at the Agency.

CHAPTER NINE

Three weeks had passed since the Board and Team started making inquiries about the Al-Qaida training camp and all but one source had reported back.

After reviewing the additional information they did have, the Board had decided the Project was too risky and started to consider alternative Projects.

Two days after the decision was made, Swabbie, Jar Head, and Doggie returned after contacting their source and met with JJ and Mac.

The following morning, JJ had the Board in session, the

Al-Qaida training camp Project was reopened, and after a long discussion, it was decided since the Team was already aware of it, the new findings would be presented to the Team for their consideration.

Before leaving for the city that morning, Mac informed JC that there was a good possibility he would be calling a meeting for that afternoon and would like everyone to attend.

By mid-afternoon, JJ brought his Jaguar to a stop in front of the Barn. He and Mac got out of the car and went inside. JC was waiting and informed them everyone was already assembled and the three men proceeded to the Team meeting room.

Upon entering, JJ went to the front of the room while Mac and JC took a seat with the Team. "Good afternoon all and thank you for being available for this meeting," JJ started. "Called you all together for an update on the Project we had already decided against: the Al-Qaida training camp in South America.

"Due to the information Swabbie, Jar Head, and Doggie supplied, we have reopened the Project for re-evaluation purposes. As you know, the normal SOP is for the Board to do an evaluation and approval process prior to passing it onto you for your evaluation and approval. This time, since everyone already knows about the Project and the reason we originally decided to bypass it, the Team and Board will perform this process at the same time. That said, I'll share the new information.

"As we all know, the training camp attendees all look like American or European types. That points to their obvious objective of wanting them to blend in when traveling in the West and the new information may explain why.

"Two of the main concerns involving terrorist attacks on the West these days are nuclear or biological and the new information points to the latter. At this time, we don't know where or when the attack will occur, but we do know if this was part of the plan at the camp on the Afghanistan—Pakistan border and was just transferred to this new camp, the lead time may be short. If it is something new, then obviously it will probably be longer depending how involved their plans are.

"As I stated, we don't know where or when the attack or attacks will take place, but we do know where they are now and we could act, but that leads us right back to the reason we bypassed on it the first time, the possibility someone is just setting a trap.

"The Board reopened the Project, but we don't want you to feel obligated during your consideration process to accept it. I know I don't have to say this next thing, but I want to. Don't forget, it may be part of an elaborate plan to draw whoever they are after into a trap.

"Now that I have brought you all up to date, I'll turn the meeting over to Mac for the operational portion," JJ concluded. As Mac started to get up from his seat, JC advised in a low voice, "The troops are in one of those moods."

"I think I can handle the situation, Colonel!" Mac replied.

"Yes, sir, General, sir," JC replied, giving him a little salute.

JJ heard the end of the exchange and said to JC, "For some reason, he has been snapping everyone off for the past two days."

When Mac got to the front of the room, he wasted no time before starting the briefing. "Afternoon all," he started. "As everyone knows, we are considering another Project in South America. This time, it's a small island off the coast of…"

"Excuse me!" JC interrupted. "You mentioning South America brought a question back to mind concerning the Project in Chile. You made a statement during that briefing about Easter Island being off the coast and you were sure everyone knew what that island was famous for, but there seemed to be some disagreement within the Team. Did we ever get that resolved?"

There was no way the Team was going to let this opportunity pass by and before Mac could reply, Panda said, "It's where the Easter Bunny lives."

"Wrong again," Jockey complained. "It's where they make all of the Easter baskets."

Mac looked at JC who was sporting a big smile then he got the Team back under control. "I think that was resolved when I explained about the huge boulders on Easter Island and the mystery about how they were moved and put in a row along the shore line."

"I remember now," Panda acknowledged. "The Easter Bunny's older brother, Big Bunny moved them."

"In a giant Easter basket," Jockey added and the Team was again laughing.

Mac looked at JC who gave him a little salute.

After again getting the Teams under control, Mac got back to the Project at hand. "I'm going to now say the name of the island; everyone will recognize the name and its history. I would personally appreciate it if no one would make that stupid ass remark one usually hears when the topic comes up." Mac paused, as he looked at the group and everyone seemed to respect his wishes. "The Island of Tortuga will be the location of the Project if it is approved by everyone." Mac again paused expecting some sort of outburst, but was surprised when the Team remained quiet. Mac knew he had gotten his message across and had the Team under control so he continued the briefing.

After covering a lot of material, he asked, "Are there any questions?"

Panda raised his hand and inquired, "Isn't the Island of Tortuga where Henry Morgan the pirate used to operate from?"

Mac answered with a headshake as he answered, "Yes."

Jockey then raised his hand. "Then the stupid ass remark you were talking about must be the word Yar! What do the rest of you think?" Jockey inquired to everyone and a gigantic, "YAR!" filled the room, as everyone replied in unison.

"Will we be the pirates or the other guys?" Panda inquired.

"Well, in that movie that was just out, the Pirate Captain had the last name of a bird and we have a Blue Jay on staff, so we'll be the pirates," Jockey suggested and the Team responded with another, "YAR!"

"He'll need a first name. How about Richard? Captain Richard Blue Jay," Panda proposed.

"How about Captain Dick," Jockey suggested.

With everyone, including Blue Jay, laughing and saying, "YAR!" after each one-liner, Mac gave up and again looked at JC.

"I usually go for coffee when this happens," JC informed him.

The fact that JC was the instigator of it all and now acting as if he was an innocent bystander snapped Mac out of his bad mood. He started to laugh then walked toward JC. "You have a spare coffee cup?"

The Team responded the same way as when JC left the room in the middle of a briefing and all followed suit with coffee cups in hand.

———

Both the Board and Team held meetings daily for the next four days dissecting the Project and considering the 'what ifs.'

What if the biological part was just info they floated out there, but it really doesn't exist? What if it does exist, but is just part of a plan to trap them? What if the biological do exist and has nothing to do with them and it is aimed at the U.S. or Europe?

If the latter was true and they didn't try to stop it, the results could be devastating. The first two days, the Teams were serious and focused, but on days three and four, they were intense.

On the fifth day, the Board made their decision and that afternoon, JJ once again had everyone in the Team meeting room at the Barn. "Good afternoon, everyone. This will be a very short meeting," JJ started. "I just wanted to inform you all of the Board's decision on the Project we have all been considering.

"The new information about a possible biological attack being planned was very compelling. Unfortunately, we had no way of confirming it was true and were left with the possibility that it is just another part of an elaborate trap. With that in mind, the Board voted to again pass on the Project. Are there any questions or comments?" JJ inquired.

With that invitation, JC spoke up. "As you know, the Team has also been holding meetings about the Project and I would like to present our findings."

"Mac and I would like to hear them," JJ approved and motioned JC to the front of the room.

"Why do I know this is going to be something bad?" General Mac inquired to JC in a low voice.

JC just smiled and shrugged his shoulders.

"Still say I liked you better when you were a captain," Mac again informed him.

JC waited until JJ had taken the seat next to Mac then started his briefing. "Usually only the Team would meet to consider a Project. This one has turned out to be very unusual, so as on other occasions, we invited the House Team, Swabbie, Jar Head, and Doggie to attend the meetings and I'm afraid we see things a little differently than the

Board," JC informed JJ and Mac. "We had come to the same conclusions as the Board at first, but then we revisited everything and unlike the Board, we had people contributing firsthand information about the reliability and character of the person that supplied the new information. Bottom line is, for the past two days, we have been planning the operational part of the Project to be presented to the Board for consideration."

JJ was caught off guard by the announcement and looked at Mac for his reaction.

Mac was just sitting there with a smile on his face. "The lad has always been trouble and now he has all of these others that are cut from the same cloth."

"I'd like to say I am surprised by their decision, but I can't," JJ replied. "They seem to have this uncontrollable need to put themselves between the terrorists and innocent people, regardless of the danger."

JJ could have tried to make a case about why they may be making a big mistake, but decided to save his breath. As in the past, they would be very courteous and listen to his words, but it wouldn't change anything, so instead he said, "Let's hear the plan. I hope it includes a strategy for presenting it to the Board."

"Would you like me to cover that part first?" JC inquired.

"Whatever!" JJ replied, shaking his head, and trying to hold back a smile.

When JC had completed the presentation, he asked for JJ and Mac's thoughts about the plan.

Mac was the first to reply. "If I said the plan was ambitious, I would be lying. This is way beyond ambitious."

"And it will be a very hard sell to the Board. The resources alone are huge," JJ added. "In the past, the Board did not even flinch when they heard the cost, but in those cases, they had approved the Projects. This time, you will be trying to reverse their decision about the Al-Qaida training camp and then have them fund it."

The meeting turned out not to be a short one as JJ had predicted, but instead, continued for hours.

Big Face was also having problems concerning the Al-Qaida training camp. When the plan was originally hatched, it was to use the training camp to draw in and destroy whoever was responsible for disrupting his plans for Central / South America and he didn't really care about the fate of the Al-Qaida training camp.

The plan to help establish the training camp close to the U.S. was completed and information about the camp was allowed to leak out that was bound to draw in the group they were trying to destroy.

Everything seemed to going as planned with the trap ready to spring when Big Face got some unexpected news.

When the idea for the trap was presented, he had estimated in the timeframe it took to establish the camp, leak out information about its existence, and the destruction of the group they were after, the terrorists would not have enough time to execute any major terrorist plots.

After the training camp had served its purpose, to show the world he was not supporting the terrorists and was still king of Central and South America, he would order the destruction of the training camp by his own military. The plan seemed reasonable, but things could get out of control when dealing with these terrorist types and Big Face was now experiencing that firsthand.

He and his people knew about the Al-Qaida training camp on the Afghanistan—Pakistan border, the American / European looking trainees, and that was what had made the idea even more appealing.

What they didn't know was Al-Qaida's closely guarded secret to use these trainees as part of a biological attack on the U.S. and that they had transplanted the camp to the Island of Tortuga with all plans basically intact, and after an adjustment to the schedule, were back on course.

Upon hearing about the planned biological attack, Big Face asserted himself through his contact with the terrorists and told them to stop planning for the attack.

Their reply was, "Do not try to dictate to Al-Qaida or your country will suffer the same fate as the American dogs."

This put Big Face in a tough spot. If the attack was carried out and any part of it was traced back to him, at the very least, he would be on the run for the remainder of his life and he couldn't ask anyone for help for the same reason.

After many secret meetings with his inner circle, it was decided a special unit of the military would move on the camp, destroy it, and he would take credit for eliminating the terrorist threat. If his country was attacked with a biological weapon, Big Face would do what he was very good at, putting a spin on things, play up the fact his country was the victim of terrorism, and both the East and West would come to his aid.

The one item that still had to be resolved was what to do about the biological weapons after his military unit disposed of the camp.

CHAPTER TEN

The Board and Team were also struggling with the problem of how to handle and dispose of the biologicals.

Dunn had met with Di Flippi about the matter and Di stated he would like to get a sample of the biological agent so he could have it analyzed to see what they were up against. He could not officially assign Agency or Agency contract personnel without giving an explanation to his superiors about where the hazmat team would be sent and why. Not being able to do either, that option was out.

He did tell Dunn he had an idea about how to get a sample into Agency hands, but had to give it more thought.

The Teams were in session at their daily morning meetings that were held during the planning stage of a Project and were reviewing the main objectives. "Now, for how we are going to handle the biological agents," JC announced the next topic. "The only other time we had to deal with hazardous material was Polonium 210. We intercepted it in transport and were reasonably sure it was safe, but as a precautionary measure, Jar Head and Doggie wore hazmat suits until they got it secured in a safe container.

"This time I don't think it will be that cut and dry," he acknowledged, as he looked in Jar Head and Doggie's direction.

"Cut and dry," Jar Head echoed his words then inquired to Doggie, "Is that what he said?"

"Yeah, that's what he said. I guess if you don't count the bad guy threatening to set off an explosive device in the briefcase carrying the Polonium 210, Wildman disregarding the treat, and putting a round between the bad guy's horns BEFORE we had on our hazmat suits, it was cut and dry," Doggie explained.

"You're still here aren't you?" JC said with a smile, remembering the incident then continued with the meeting.

"I know everyone has been giving a lot of thought to this part of the Project, but does anyone have anything?"

"We may have something." Top Kiner spoke up. "I know a man; I'll call him Major Tex for now. He served in the Marine Corps, has up to date hazmat training, and can be trusted."

"We can vouch for him," Lady1 spoke up. "He had worked with our husbands on different occasions and they both trusted him."

"They were active in clandestine activities within the intelligence community that brought people from different agencies and units from the military together for a particular mission then were disbanded. With his hazmat knowledge, he would be an ideal candidate," LadyA added.

"Sounds good," JC acknowledged. "I'll pass it onto JJ and Mac. If the Board gives the okay, they'll check him out.

"We will now revisit how we are going to orchestrate the securing of the camp, locate any biologicals onsite, and how we are going to conceal our identities to the hazmat people while they deal with the biologicals."

———

Not knowing the terrorists' timetable for a possible attack on the U.S., the Board and Team were dedicating a lot of time to the Project. A decision was made to bring on Major Tex, but it was obvious a second man should be added to work with him.

This was still an outstanding issue the next time Dunn had one of his meetings with Di Flippi.

"I've also personally ran very discreet inquires about your Major Tex and have decided the House Team has made an excellent recommendation," Di started. "As for the outstanding issue of the second man, I have a recommendation. I'm sure you remember the Navy Seal we brought onboard for the Polonium 210 Project?"

Dunn shook his head in agreement before Di got to the question, already knowing it was another excellent choice.

For the Polonium 210 Project, a person not connected with the Teams was required. Per Admiral Fox's recommendation and after being checked out, a Navy Seal was recruited. He performed very well and had since joined Di Flippi's staff at the Agency.

Since his only contact during that Project was Di Flippi, it seemed obvious it was a CIA operation. He was never told any differently and better yet, he never questioned Di about the operation.

"So we're in agreement then?" Di Flippi inquired.

"Very much so," Gil replied.

"Good. I also have a recommendation on how to handle the biologicals—in the same manner we did for the Polonium 210. I will be the only contact for the Seal and Major Tex making disposing of the hazardous material look like an Agency operation."

Gil again shook his head in agreement then said, "You are certainly volunteering a lot these days."

"It must be the area. Every time we meet in the area of Pickets Charge, I get in volunteer mode. I know if the bureaucrats and politicians get on to what I have been doing, they'll have my ass, but I do it anyway."

"So you see yourself in the same class as those brave men that made the charge that day?" Dunn inquired, paused, then added, "Now I don't quite see it that way. To me, it's more like you saying, 'If I dood it, I get a whippin.' I dood it anyway.'"

Di looked at Gil and said, "You never have gotten out of that DDO big pain in the ass mode, have you? You know I never did like you."

Dunn started laughing and as always inquired, "Never?"

"Never!" was the quick reply.

"Come on, I'll buy you dinner," Gil invited, "sort of like the condemned man's last good meal."

"Nope, I don't want you paying for my food with gun runner money," Di replied, referring to Dunn being president of a firearms company. "I'll bet you sell to Castro and Big Face don't you? But then that may be a good thing. How dangerous can they be using that shit that you manufacture?"

Gil hadn't seen him fired up like this in a very long time and was enjoying every minute of it. He knew when Di got on a roll, you were in for many laughs and as the two men made their way back to where their cars were parked, Di had to keep reminding Dunn to hold down the noise.

———

Since the meeting at Gettysburg, Di Flippi had spoken with the Seal about the mission, and met with and recruited the Major.

After Major Tex and the Seal met, they started training together. The Seal's primary responsibility would be security, Major Tex the biologicals, and he would also conduct Hazmat 101 class in case a backup was required.

Needless to say after the first day, the Navy— Marine Corps adversarial humor broke out and the two men became friends very quickly.

———————

The Team was informed Major Tex and the Seal were added to handle the biologicals and everyone studied photos of the two men.

At the Barn, it was planning in the morning then training in the afternoon. One afternoon, as the Team was filing out of the Barn to go for an afternoon run, they came across JC, Jockey, and Mac trying to get a pulley system they had rigged up to work properly, but weren't having much success.

The Team stopped and watched for a while, then Panda said, "Witnessed something like this at the zoo one time when I saw three monkeys trying to fuck a football."

The Team responded with a group, "YAR!" and laughter then continued to their afternoon run, as the three men responded with a barrage of verbal abuse.

———————

Big Face wasn't having as much success with his plans, mainly due to him wanting to have the main say about everything.

Planning included moving the force that was in place for the trap further away from the terrorist camp to avoid any clashes between the terrorists and that force.

A special military unit to take out the camp was ready, but the biologicals became a stumbling block and finally, out of frustration, Big Face decided fire was the only answer and that after everyone was killed, the camp would be put to the torch.

———————

With preparations completed, the Team was ready to depart and after a last minute check, got into their vehicles. The same procedure for the trip would be used. The van carrying all of their weapons and other gear concealed in hidden compartments would be driven by JC. Two other vehicles, one in front and one a short distance behind the van would make the trip to Mercer Airport in West Trenton, New Jersey.

The initial part of the morning trip was uneventful, as the three vehicles made a left turn at Brookville, then traveled south on Route 29 and several miles later, passed the city limits of a small town nested along the Delaware River. It was early morning and to avoid looking like a convoy, about half a block past the Lambertville Police Department Headquarters, the lead vehicle made a right turn onto Cherry Street, proceeded to Union Street where it turned left, passed Body Tech Fitness and continued heading south. The van continued on Main Street with the third vehicle a short distance behind.

The van paced its progress to allow the vehicle running parallel on Union Street to keep up or get a little ahead. When the vehicles reached Bridge Street, they both had to stop for red lights and communicated that to each other.

When the lights turned green, JC was very slow to react and pretended he was observing something at Cifelli's Sunoco Station on the corner of Bridge and Main Streets.

While the van paused, the vehicle on Union crossed over Bride Street, passed the Wonderful World of Wines liquor store, and continued south. At the end of Union Street, it made a left turn, then a quick right. Since they were the lead vehicle, they were wasting no time as they proceeded down Wilson Street.

"Watch that vehicle!" Benz advised, as he observed a lady starting to get out of her car in front of a white building.

Bean had already noticed her and was taking evasive action to avoid an accident.

"No problem," Benz advised, as he observed the lady, then the letters on the front door of the building as they passed by.

"Sorry, lady," Bean said, as he looked into the rearview mirror and gave a wave.

No damage was done, but the speeding car had startled the lady and she responded accordingly.

"Hello!" Bean chuckled. "She just made a gesture."

Benz laughed and added, "And I'll bet you will be the main topic of conversation at the YMAC today as well."

Bean proceeded to Feeder Street and held position where he could see the oncoming traffic on Route 29. When the van approached, he pulled onto the road and was again the lead vehicle, as they passed the River Walk office complex.

Route 29 changes from four lanes back to two at the Lambertville City limits and as JC passed ED Towle's Auto Repair Shop, a vehicle containing four men started to pass then quickly slowed down and pulled in behind the van just as the four lanes became two.

"What do we have here?" Bris inquired who was driving the trailing vehicle.

"Let's just wait and see what they have in mind," JC instructed over the com units.

"I'd say they are planning to follow the van to its destination and with just one old fuck in the truck, how hard will it be to hijack it?" an anonymous voice said over the com.

JC just smiled. He recognized the voice and would respond in time. Maybe not today, but in time.

The vehicles proceeded down Route 29 and were approaching Scutters Falls Bridge when JC came on the com. "When I make a turn up ahead, you people keep going."

No one questioned why, they just gave confirmation that they had gotten the message.

Shortly after getting the message, Bean took the slight turn to the right that put him onto old Route 29 and the other three vehicles followed. After traveling a short distance, JC put on his turn signal then made a left turn into a driveway and started up a long hill. The car with the four men started to follow until they saw the big sign that read, New Jersey State Police Division Headquarters, then quickly changed their minds, swung back onto the road, and picked up speed as they departed.

"Good move," Bris commended, as he passed the same driveway.

"More than one way to shake off fleas," JC replied, as he made a left turn into the parking lot of a small building halfway up the long hill. After making a wide swing, the van was back at the driveway, made a right turn, then a left, and he was again on the way to Mercer Field and the waiting Global Express business jet.

CHAPTER ELEVEN

The Global Express business jet had landed at the International Airport on Bonaire, an island in the Dutch Antilles, and Jockey was taxiing it to a remote part of the airport where another business jet and several other aircraft were parked.

As with prior Projects, the Board had handled all logistical matters making sure not to leave a trace or a paper trail that led to nowhere.

When the Global Express came to a stop, everyone deplaned, Jockey and JC went to check out a C-295 cargo aircraft that was parked nearby, and were shortly joined by Bean and Blue Jay.

"Ready to take it for a test drive?" Bean inquired.

"Just about," Jockey answered, as he and JC made some final checks.

While JC and the other Team members made preparations for the upcoming events, Jockey would fly Bean and Blue Jay over to the British Virgin Islands to meet with an old friend of theirs and try to get additional information about Tortuga.

In the early 90s, The Brit worked for MI6. He was stationed in Jamaica and went way out on a limb to help Blue Jay and Bean to complete a personal mission. He still worked for intelligence and was now the MI6 man on The British Virgin Islands.

There was no question about trusting him and he usually played a lone hand. If he felt Home Office needed to know something, they would, if not, they wouldn't and had proven that in the past. If he had reported to Home Office what Blue Jay and Bean were up to, the duo would probably now be in prison or on the run.

For that matter, if the whole story were known, all three of them would be sharing the same fate.

When checking out the plane was completed, Jockey informed the duo that they could depart and the three men started to board the plane.

"Sure you don't want me to fly you over there?" JC inquired. "I don't want you children to get lost. Your pilot has a bad sense of direction especially over water and at Pussy Airways, they didn't teach much in the way of instrument flying."

"Let's think about this," Jockey requested. "Does anyone recall some of his flying? How about that landing in the desert when the plane was full of explosives? That was fun!"

Blue Jay and Bean saw where this was going and wanted to meet with The Brit some time in the near future, so they both started pushing Jockey up the rear ramp and into the plane.

"Ya big sissy," JC replied. "I considered that a combat situation."

"Ho yeah, well, let's talk about how the JC Crazy Fuck Award came about," Jockey's voiced echoed out the back of the plane, as the duo pushed him toward the cockpit.

It was quiet for a few seconds until JC looked into the back of the plane with a big smile on his face. "But that's just the opinion of the old fuck in the truck." Then added, "You people be careful."

"It's cake," Jockey replied. "We'll be back in no time."

Humorous jousting was the norm for the Teams and if it didn't occur on a regular basis, it became a concern as to why.

———

By the time Bean and Blue Jay arrived at a place close to the airfield where they were to meet with The Brit, it was afternoon. He was nowhere to be found, but both knew he was probably already in the area and checking things out before he made an appearance.

The two lit up cigars, but didn't have to wait long before they heard, "I say, aren't they supposed to be bad for your health?" The Brit inquired, appearing out of nowhere.

Seeing Blue Jay and Bean were a little surprised, he explained, "Been stationed here for a while, know most of the nooks and crannies," then added, "good to see you chaps again. I believe the last time was Cuba 94 wasn't it?" he inquired.

Fifteen years had passed since he had seen the duo. People do change in appearance and the question was for verification purposes.

"And the real answer is…" Bean started.

"Jamaica 93," Blue Jay finished.

"Quite so," The Brit said with a smile. "But I do remember the humor." With that, the three men burst into laughter and greeted each other properly.

"What are you chaps up to this time?" The Brit inquired.

"Looking for information about the Island of Tortuga," Blue Jay answered.

"The island itself or the Al-Qaida group that set up shop there?" he replied with a smile.

"I'm starting to remember the humor myself," Bean volunteered.

"I wasn't supposed to, but popped over there when I first got wind that Al-Qaida might be in the area. One wants to keep up you know?"

"One does," Blue Jay assured him.

"When I was there, they seemed to have set up shop in a large cave on the island, but haven't been back for a closer look. Figured I would give them some time to get started with whatever they had in mind."

"We know about the cave," Blue Jay informed him. "Do you have any info about their security or the area in general?"

The Brit then proceeded to give the duo all of the information he had gathered during his visit to

the island plus some other tidbits he had accumu-
lated.

After he had given all of the information and
answered their questions, he inquired, "Is this an
official outing or are you chaps on another personal mission?"

"Good question," Bean said, as he and Blue
Jay looked at each other.

The Brit seeing the look said, "Understand,
need to know and all of that," realizing he had put
them into an awkward position.

"Thank you for understanding," Blue Jay
said, then followed with, "Bean and I want to
again thank you for Jamaica. We know you went
way out on a limb to help us."

"Wasn't much. Just loaned you some scuba
equipment and other odds and ends," he said,
downplaying his importance.

"We think it was more than that," Bean spoke
up. "When we were running for our lives, some of
the bad guys were dropping for no apparent reason."

"Really?" was the one word reply.

"We, too, understand, need to know and all of
that," Blue Jay spoke up.

"Jolly good," The Brit answered with a smile.

Having the reason for the meeting satisfied,
the three talked about Jamaica and other topics
until the duo had to return to the airfield and the
flight back to Bonaire.

CHAPTER TWELVE

The Island of Tortuga was a good choice. With the exception of a few fishermen during lobster season, it was uninhabited. It was an ideal place to establish a terrorist camp, create biological weapons, or if you just wanted to set a trap for someone and wipe them out without anyone being around to get in the way or ask questions later.

Jockey maintained an altitude of 3,000 feet as the C-295 approached the island.

The Team members were busy preparing four weighted down dummies that would act as one of the decoys in case there were people on the island waiting to ambush the Team.

The plan was to push out the dummies as the plane flew over the shoreline. The weight of each dummy was 150 pounds for two reasons. First, if they were too light, they wouldn't pull the parachutes down and who knows where they would end up. Second, the plan was for the parachutes to be caught by the land breeze that should be coming off the island at that hour and carry the chutes out to sea.

Everyone knows landing in water is dangerous; a person can get tangled in the lines and drowned, and that was the illusion the Team was trying to accomplish. A four-man unit attempted a pre-dawn jump onto the island. They were pushed out to sea and drowned.

"Get ready back there," JC instructed on the com and the dummies were carried to the back of the plane, as Tic lowered the rear ramp of the C-295.

Jockey wasn't trying to set any speed records, as the plane lumbered along as it approached the beach.

"Coming up on drop zone," JC again informed and the Team members got a firm grip on the dummies.

Two men per dummy were lined up in a row. When they got the word, the first two men followed by the others would proceed to the ramp, throw out their dummy, then would step aside to allow the other men to do the same. The chutes would open automatically within five seconds and if there were no malfunctions, float down hopefully into the sea.

"On my mark," JC alerted, shortly followed by, "Do it," and within seconds, the first dummy started its trip followed by the other three.

Tic was intently watching to make sure each chute opened and 10 seconds after the last dummy went out, he reported into the com, "All chutes opened. No malfunctions and looking good."

Jockey maintained the lumbering pace of the plane, so they could see if their plan about the land breeze would work.

As the 150 pounds pulled the chutes down, Tic was still intently watching. At first, it looked like the opposite was going to happen when the chutes started drifting inland, but at a lower altitude, they reversed and starting drifting toward the sea.

"It looks like it's going to work. They just passed over the beach and my guess is they'll go in a few hundred yards off the beach," Tic reported.

"Good work. Now let's hope someone was down there to witness all of our clever planning in action," JC replied.

After Tic's report, Jockey pushed the throttles full forward and after clearing the island, he dropped down to 1,000 feet as the plane headed out to sea. He would keep this course for a short time then start to come around and head for the real jump site.

As the plane navigated toward the drop zone, Jockey was on the com unit. "JC, I'm getting a little confused. Now the first drop was inland and the second is along the beach, so the dummies will go into the water, right?"

"I'm not sure myself, but both cases involve dummies, so you have that part correct," JC replied from the co-pilot's seat as both men smiled.

Several comments from the Team were immediately heard over the com and when everything quieted down, JC said, "I'm picking up static on my com, how about you?"

"Yeah, I am, too. Maybe the Team is trying to contact us from the island. I'll swing around after we drop these dummies."

As the plane approached the drop zone, JC appeared in the back of the plane and pretended to be surprised when he saw the Team. "Hey, Jockey, the Team is still onboard!"

"Really, I hope we're at the right jump zone," Jockey replied.

"If it is or isn't, it's still safer out there than in here with Crazy and the man from Pussy Airways," Panda informed everyone.

JC was still chuckling as he put his hand on the lever to lower the rear ramp in preparation for the jump when he said into the com unit, "You people be extra careful down there. I know I say this every time, but it is especially true this time. If it becomes too dangerous to complete the Project, back off. We'll get them another day."

"Ditto," Jockey's voice echoed over the com.

The Team knew their words were sincere and appreciated it. They had become like family with the same concerns that come with being family.

A few seconds later, Jockey advised, "Coming up on drop zone," and JC lowered the ramp. The Team moved to the back of the plane and prepared to jump. "Good Luck," JC wished everyone.

"Good luck," Jockey again echoed followed by, "on my mark," and 20 seconds later said, "Do it." The Team started down the ramp then into midair.

This was a low altitude jump and the team members immediately started checking out the landing zone in the morning light for safe places to land.

"Count nine chutes, no malfunctions," JC reported over the com.

The plane continued lumbering along until they got word from the ground that everyone had landed safely then Jockey pushed the throttles full forward to pick up speed for their return trip to Bonaire.

———————

The Team had concealed their chutes, quickly left the drop zone, and had regrouped a short distance away.

While the Team made sure the area was secure, Blue Jay calculated their exact location and consulted a map of the island he had spread on the ground. Having secured the area, Blue Jay assembled the Team around the map and after making them aware of their location and the location of their objective, Blue Jay reviewed their route and how the objective would be approached.

———————

As the Team reviewed how they would be moving toward their objective, three high-speed boats were approaching a beach on the south side of the island away from the dummy and actual drop zones.

Top Kiner and Swabbie manned the first boat with LadyA and Doggie in the second, and Lady1 and Jar Head in the third.

Not knowing if or where an enemy force might be located, the dummy drop and the three boats were two planned diversions. The boats would hold at their position until notified to move to the next location.

As the three boats approached the beach, they all reduced their speed until they were barely making forward progress as Swabbie, Doggie, and Jar Head scanned the entire area with binoculars.

"All seems quiet," Jar Head said into his com unit and the other two agreed.

The three boats increased their speed a little until they were at the beach then cut their engines and let the bottoms of the three crafts come to rest gently on the white sand.

The plan was for the six to take up positions that formed a fan and wait. Taking different angles, the members of each boat would cross the beach and advance. When they decided the boats and shoreline could not be seen if they advanced any further, one would stay at that position and the other would continue on before stopping making sure they did not lose sight of the other person.

Their objective was not to engage, but to detect any force approaching their positions, inform the others, and all would quickly return to the beach and leave the area.

The ladies had their hair tucked up under floppy camouflaged hats giving the impression that six men were on the beach. If they made a hasty retreat, it might be determined by an approaching force that they retreated because they were discovered or that these six couldn't establish communications with the other four, realized something had happened, and that the mission was a wash.

Leaving their boats and quickly crossing the beach, the six paused and again checked out the area before continuing on.

With the sea already covering 180 degrees of their position, the group proceeded to cover the remaining 180. Top and Swabbie took a straight course while the other four proceeded at left or right angles.

When all six got into position, a total calm returned and the only thing that could be heard were small waves lapping the boats and the beach.

CHAPTER THIRTEEN

After attaching the local vegetation to their ghillie suits, the Team moved out and was traveling quickly, but at the same time, being very cautious as they moved toward their objective.

The combination of ghillie suits, cammies, and skill enabled the Team to blend into the landscape at will. Since they had been working together as a unit for over seven years, it looked more like a directed scene from a movie than a real life situation.

It would take several hours for the Team to get to a point where they would change from traveling quickly to snooping and pooping as they moved in close to their objective.

The Board members had just finished breakfast on a yacht they had rented the week prior and were on deck drinking coffee when Foxie joined them. "So far, so good," he told the others. "Just got the codeword from JC that everything went well at his end. Top also reported their group was in position."

"Onto the next phase," Mac said, as he stood up, proceeded toward the back of the yacht, and the task he had started earlier.

"Know I'm probably going to regret saying this. Do you want some help?" Wilson asked.

"You know something about pulleys? Weed Whacker," Mac inquired, using a nickname he had given him due to his fondness for the Thompson submachine gun and what Mac jokingly said Wilson does to the weeds with it.

"I know a little something about it, Talley Whacker!" Wilson quickly replied.

"Don't get tense, Wilson, just kidding. Would appreciate your help," Mac told him and both men along with the others proceeded to the makeshift pulley system Mac was setting up.

The Team made good time. They were now moving slower as they approached the area where the Al-Qaida camp was located and Blue Jay had brought them to a halt while he checked for the best way to approach their objective.

The Brit had told them about booby traps he had encountered during his visit and their locations were in obvious lanes of attack if someone were to assault the camp.

As Blue Jay continued to survey the camp, Bean inquired over the com, "I wonder if there is any pirate treasure buried around here?"

"Why don't you start to dig and find out?" Blue Jay suggested.

"If I found a big chest full of jewels and gold, I bet it would be worth over two million dollars," Bean wondered aloud, "and that would amount to about one hundred forty thousand dollars for each member of the Teams."

"I say, it would be closer to one hundred forty-two thousand eight hundred and change," Pru corrected.

"Well, I'm really glad our Field Financial Advisor and Mr. Math Buster got the usual field financial report out of their systems. I was beginning to worry it might come up in the middle of a firefight or some other inopportune moment," Blue Jay remarked while he continued checking out the objective.

The plan was to engage the Al-Qaida force then use the M-79 grenade launchers to pump tear gas into the cave that should drive any terrorists out into the open. After dealing with the terrorists, the Team would check out the camp, then blend into the area, and secure the camp while the hazmat team completed their task and left the area.

The trick was going to be getting close enough to execute the plan.

As Blue Jay slowly moved his field glasses to his right, he noticed movement in the vegetation and held the binoculars on that spot. Seconds later, he saw movement again and alerted the Team.

After being given the location, Benz and Panda had their spotter scopes focused on that area and Panda reported, "They are moving low and slow whoever they are."

"I count about twenty," Benz added.

"They could be part of an Al-Qaida training exercise or a force with the same objective as us. Let's wait to see what happens," Blue Jay whispered into the com. "Break out the M82's."

While Benz and Panda kept track of the force moving in on the camp, Pru and Met removed their Barrett M82 rifles from their drag bags and started to assemble them. The weapon fired the .416 caliber round that could travel 1.4 miles in 2.3 seconds with deadly accuracy. At 500 yards, it takes less than half a second and with expert shooters like Met and Pru, a larger force can be overcome or at the very least sent ducking for cover when men are thrown into the air in quick succession when they are hit by the supersonic rounds.

Blue Jay lay very still as he continued to watch the force, but his thoughts were traveling at 100 miles an hour. *If this is a training exercise, we'll let it play out. When it has completed, everyone will probably relax as they all go to some sort of review of the exercise and that will be a good time for us to move in closer. On the other hand, if they are here to attack the camp, they are most likely men sent by Big Face and does that mean they are here to deal with the terrorists and there isn't a plan to ambush the Team?* Panda interrupted his thoughts on the com. "Don't think this is a training exercise. There is a three-man unit way to the rear and one has what looks like a flamethrower strapped to his back."

Now knowing what the force was about to do, Blue Jay was on the com. "Let's set up in support positions, but do not engage. If the attacking force is successful and they touch the camp, we'll withdraw with no samples, but the threat will have been neutralized.

"If things don't work out that way, we'll take advantage of the situation. Same objectives, but instead of trying to get in very close before attacking, we'll hit them as they return to camp.

"Hopefully, at their level of training, someone will have to instruct them to set up in defense and that delay will work to our advantage. Pru and Met will add to that delay as they take out whoever is acting like a leader."

The Team was listening to his instructions as they moved into support positions. They didn't require detailed instructions; they just needed to know the game plan.

As they watched the force move toward the camp, Panda inquired over the com, "Benz, check out the area at ten o'clock in front of that group. Think I saw a little movement in the brush, but if I did, it's now stationary."

Benz swung his spotter scope to 10 o'clock and started scanning very slowly back and forth. "I see him," Benz finally replied. "He may be security for the camp or a point man for that force."

At that point, with no way to verify, Blue Jay decided to wait. Regardless whose side the man was on, if they took the shot, the force moving of the camp would know someone else was in the area and he didn't want to make the Team's presence know yet.

———————

As the drama played out at the camp, Major Tex and the Seal had also held up in an area about a quarter mile from the camp after Blue Jay had alerted them to the situation. They would hold that position until they were advised to move up to get a sample of the biologicals then destroy the rest.

"It's too quiet," the Seal observed.

"It usually is before all hell breaks loose," Major Tex replied.

"True, true," the Seal agreed, as he continued to scan the surrounding area.

CHAPTER FOURTEEN

The spotters and long range shooters were glued to the unfolding situation while the rest of the Team made sure someone wasn't sneaking up on their positions when Benz commented, "This guy is either their point man, a very cool bad guy, or he's suicidal because they're almost on top of him."

No sooner were the words spoken when the man in question opened fire with an automatic weapon killing the first two men of the approaching force before he was taken out by the others.

The man must have been in communications with the camp because when the shooting started, 30 men came over the ridge to the right and attacked the force. With automatic weapons firing from both sides, a fierce firefight broke out and the terrorists seemed to be getting the upper hand.

"Looks like plan B for us," Blue Jay informed the others. "There are more assholes in this camp than we figured, so Benz and Panda will join in assaulting the camp. Are you two okay with not having your spotters?" he asked Pru and Met.

"No problem," they both agreed.

"You know the drill," Blue Jay continued. "When we hit the terrorists, you two first take out the leaders or whoever tries to be a leader. Questions anyone? Let's move out."

The firefight raged on as the Team moved toward the camp. Tic and Check were carrying M-79 grenade launchers that could fire an assortment of rounds including tear gas and high explosives.

When they got to what looked like a good place to intercept the Al-Qaida force as they returned to the camp area, Blue Jay halted the Team. "Tic, Check, Bris, get a decent angle to fire the gas grenades into the cave, the rest of us will set up here," was the only thing he had to say and everyone knew what to do. "How's the firefight going?" he then inquired to Pru and Met.

"The Home Team have the visitors on the run," Met replied.

"Roger that," Blue Jay answered then inquired on the other longer range com unit he was also carrying, "Mat, are you out there?"

"About one click away," the Seal answered.

"Start moving in. We haven't been asked to dance yet, but we are planning to cut in soon."

Now knowing other forces were in the area, Major Tex and the Seal started moving very cautiously.

With the exception of the occasional gunshot, the firefight seemed to be over as, "Update," was heard over the com. "A few seemed to have managed to escape, but the wounded and captured are being executed in a party type atmosphere," Pru reported in an uncommonly serious voice.

"Well, let's see if we can crash their party mood when they get here," Blue Jay instructed.

Pru and Met were already earmarking the Al-Qaida types that were egging the others on or who were too enthusiastic in performing the slaughter. They would soon be taking a ride on the .417 express.

Tic, Check, and Bris had located a position that would allow them to fire gas rounds into the cave and also participate in the upcoming firefight.

Tic and Check had already removed the grenade launchers that were attached to their backpacks before crawling to their current positions and were laying the color-coded rounds identifying gas from high explosives on the ground next to them while Bris acted as security. They were both carrying the old single shot grenade launcher, but it was good enough for what they wanted to accomplish.

With the slaughter completed, the terrorists were heading back to camp all still on a high about the ambush, the aftermath, and were chattering a mile a minute when what sounded like a giant whisper erupted from the foliage close by.

As people started to fall within their group, the others looked to their leaders and trainers for instructions, but one by one, they were all taken out by the M-82s.

Seeing their leaders being cut down, two of the men that were too enthusiastic at the slaughter tried to take charge.

"It will be a pleasure to take out these two," Met said into the com.

"Which one do you want?" Pru inquired, still in a very serious mood and a few seconds later, the two terrorists simultaneously were thrown into the air as they took a ride on the .417 express.

When Check and Tic heard the giant whisper, they both fired tear gas rounds into the cave, re-loaded, and fired two more. It didn't take long to affect the people in the cave who came out chok-ing and desperately seeking fresh air as tears streamed down their faces.

With that task completed, the two reloaded with high explosive grenades, laid the launchers on the ground, picked up their MP5s, and the three men waited.

When the leaders of the security force that were left behind in the camp heard the AK47 fire so close, they quickly assembled their men and proceeded to aid their fellow terrorists.

As they approached the left front of the wait-ing men, Bris alerted the other two of their pres-ence.

As the excited security force moved in front of them, they were making so much noise that no one heard the pong sounds as Tic and Check fired two HE rounds. They fired both rounds at a high angle trying to place them amongst the group, then reloaded, fired again, and the three quickly ducked to avoid anything that might come flying their way. After the four rounds had exploded, they came up firing.

When the leaders of the group discovered who was bringing them under fire, they quickly got the attention of the people around them directing all to attack the area to their right flank.

When some of the men started moving in that direction, the others realized what they were doing and joined the assault.

At first, Bris, Tic, and Check were holding them at bay, but as the entire force started heading their way, it became a challenge.

Bean was at the far left of the group engaged in the other firefight and closest to the three being assaulted. He had ducked down, reloaded, and was checking on the status of the three before rejoining the fight when he saw what was happening. "The other unit needs help," Bean's voice announced into the com before he sprayed the group with his MP5.

That got the attention of a few members of the attackers, but when other men in the group started flying through the air, the rest decided the terrorists' business was a little too dangerous and started to flee.

"Good shooting," Bean praised as he, Pru, and Met rejoined the other firefight that seemed to be winding down. After a small group tried to break for the cave and was cut down by Bris, Tic, and Check, it was over.

When things got quiet, Blue Jay was on the com to Major Tex and the Seal. "Mat, you close?"

"Real," was the reply.

"Give us a minute," Blue Jay replied, then instructed into the Team's com, "Let's do a sweep."

As Pru and Met used the spotter scopes to scan the camp, parts of the surrounding area stood up and moved cautiously toward the camp. Since it was daylight and they didn't want to reveal their identities, the Team all wore hooded masks to hide their faces. The Team moved quickly through the camp as Tic, Check, and Bris checked the cave as best they could while standing outside the entrance.

After all was secured, "If you're suited up, come ahead," was heard on the com and the Major and Seal headed for the camp.

When they arrived at the site, the Team wasn't standing around in plain view, but they definitely had everything under control. After seeing all of the dead bodies, Major Tex and the Seal knew they didn't have to worry about the area not being secured.

As the two men approached the cave's entrance, Blue Jay and Bean were there to give them the status. "Gas grenades drove a gang of asses out when the firefight started. Can't blame them, that gas is nasty shit, but if someone had a gas mask handy, they could have held out. Not knowing the status of any biologicals in there, we didn't sweep the cave."

"That's all right," Major Tex replied, as he deposited his backpack, MP5, and other gear at the front of the cave. "That's what I'm here for and fish man will take care of any stragglers," he continued, referring to the Seal.

"Just hope I don't get too excited if somebody jumps up and mow your ass down by mistake," was the quick reply, as the Seal chambered a new round into his MP5.

Hearing the exchange over the com, everyone smiled and thought these two would fit right in with the Team.

With hazmat gear in one hand and a semiautomatic pistol in the other, Major Tex inquired, "Ready."

"Yeah," the Seal replied, then added, "I've got to stop getting involved in these types of things. Last time I was sneaking up on a man in a van. This time it's a cave."

"Don't worry, the big bad Marine will protect you," the Major assured him.

"You've got the big part right. It will give me something to hide behind," the Seal replied, as he started toward the cave's entrance.

After the two men disappeared into the cave, everyone kept surveying the area outside for any unwanted guests when a burst from an MP5 and two shots from the semiautomatic pistol echoed from the cave, then it got quiet again.

"Everything all right, fish man?" Bean inquired.

"Yeah, just a few turds," he replied.

"Looks like they were guarding the stuff," the Major added.

While Major Tex took a sample of the biologicals, the Seal checked out the rest of the cave and discovered a dozen briefcases lined up along the left side of the cave, but didn't investigate. The objective was to get a sample, destroy anything remaining, and depart.

Major Tex had secured the sample, sprayed the remainder with a neutralizing agent, and rejoined the Seal. "See anything interesting?" he inquired.

"I wouldn't touch anything in here with a fork," the Seal informed him.

"Don't blame you. This isn't the best lab I've ever run across," the Major replied. "After I spray it, I would like to torch this place just for good measure."

Hearing the conversation on their com, Blue Jay inquired, "I think that's what the other group had in mind. They brought a flamethrower with them and it's still out there."

"That would work," the Major replied and Blue Jay dispatched Benz and Panda to retrieve it.

After a few minutes had passed, the two men reappeared just inside the cave's entrance. The Major retrieved a spray bottle from one of the pockets of his hazmat suit and started spraying the Seal from head to toe. When he had finished, the Seal produced another bottle and did the same for the Major. That completed, the two men stepped outside the cave and started to remove their hazmat suits and discarded them back into the cave.

"Don't see any holes in your suit, Major. When we heard that MP5 burst, we were wondering!" Bean yelled out.

"It was close, but I'm quick," the Major replied.

"You're just lucky they aren't calling you Major Swiss right now," the Seal spoke up and both smiled.

As Benz and Panda moved back to retrieve the flamethrower, they asked Met and Pru if they had located it and were told it was out of their line of sight, but gave them an educated guess as to its location.

When Panda and Benz got to that location, they did a quick scan, spotted the downed man with the flamethrower, and proceeded in his direction.

When they got to the lifeless body, they removed the unit. Panda picked it up by the harness and Benz was in the process of picking up his MP5 when two men concealed in the bush dressed in camouflaged uniforms lunged out at him with knives in hand. Acting on reflex, Benz parried the attack of the first man, then grabbed the attacker's wrist, twisted it until the palm was facing the ground, and then struck the inside of the elbow with his right fist at the same time pushing the knife back into the attacker's midsection.

Panda started to assist, but suddenly had the same problem.

Swinging the flamethrower by its harness, he took out the first attacker when the tanks made full contact with the man's head.

It was too cumbersome a weapon to use on the second man, so Panda dropped it and waited for the attack that immediately followed.

The man lunged forward and thrust the point of his knife at his victim's throat, but Panda grabbed and held onto the sleeve of the attacking arm before it could do any damage. As the two men struggled, Panda quickly slipped his right arm around the attacker's neck, then in lightning quick succession, performed quick foot movements as he pulled and twisted to his left, drove his right hip into the man, and the two went airborne with Panda being on top when they landed on the ground. He then quickly put the attacker out of commission.

Benz's second attacker was more cautious than the first, as he moved around looking for an opening. Benz knew by the way that he was moving that he had experience with a knife. After moving around a little more, the man made his move and lunged for the midsection. Benz intercepted it and again grabbed the wrist, but this time, the attacker twisted his wrist until the palm was facing up and was attempting to cut his arm. Benz saw the move, threw the attacker's arm in a downward motion, grabbed the man's camouflaged top with both hands, then performed a perfect Uchi Mata, and two men were again twisting in midair and upon landing, the knife fighter was also taken out of commission.

Benz and Panda were in the process of picking up their weapons and the flamethrower when Pru's voice came over the com. "Careful, chaps, a large force just appeared about two clicks from your position."

"That explains the run-in we just had," Benz replied. "They were probably scouts from that approaching force."

"Need assistance?" Blue Jay quickly inquired.

"No, we're okay and starting back now."

"How large is that force?" Blue Jay asked.

"We're still estimating the size," Pru replied.

"That large!" Blue Jay remarked then said, "Major, have an idea that force is looking for us, so it might be best for you to leave as soon as possible for your pickup coordinates."

Blue Jay then removed a map from his pocket, unfolded it, knelt down, and spread it on the ground. He then consulted with Pru about the location of the approaching force.

———

What Pru and Met didn't see was the Al-Qaida sniper who had arrived ahead of the big force, made a wide swing around the area, and was now set up on the other side of the camp.

———

When Big Face decided to destroy the Al-Qaida camp, he instructed the large force that was in place for the ambush to be moved five miles from the camp area. He figured if the big force were discovered, it would eliminate the element of surprise for the special force he was sending to destroy the camp.

The precaution was a little too late. The force had already been discovered, an Al-Qaida sniper was assigned to watch the force, and report their movements. When the force moved, so did the sniper.

This day, when the large force started to move and the sniper got no response on the radio from the camp, he knew something was wrong and arrived back in the area way ahead of the large force.

Seeing what had happened, he started scanning for targets of opportunity, mainly the people in charge.

The sniper had selected his first target; the man kneeling down looking at something spread out on the ground and was getting into position for his first shot.

———

The Seal and Major carefully removed their gloves halfway then tossed them back into the cave.

When Blue Jay stood up and motioned for them to join him, the sniper lost his shot.

While attempting to reacquire the target, he noticed two men walking from the cave area. One was carrying a container and the sniper took a moment to re-evaluate his target selection.

The container might have a sample of the biologicals from the cave and would be a higher priority target. The man with the container became his new target and he started to stalk his new prey.

The Major and Seal joined Blue Jay who pointed to a location on the map where the large force was approaching from and the route the Team was going to take.

Major Tex and the Seal pointed to their pickup point then what seemed to be the best route for them to take when they departed.

All agreed, Blue Jay folded up the map and said, "You people better get started. We'll burn out the cave before we leave." He then inquired into the com, "Are you people getting close?"

"Almost there," Panda answered.

"Long range shooters, keep me advised," were Met and Pru's instructions to keep him updated about the progress of that force.

The Seal and Major were ready to move out and approached Bean and Blue Jay before departing. "Good luck," they both wished, as they shook hands with the other two.

"Enjoyed working with you," Blue Jay advised them.

"You fit right in with our group," Bean added.

All shook their heads in agreement knowing what Bean meant by his statement.

As the Major and Seal disappeared on the other side of the camp, they were not alone. The sniper figured he would get two kills plus whatever was in the container.

———

When Benz and Panda appeared with the flamethrower, they headed straight for the cave. The two were breathing hard when they reached the cave, so Bean took the flamethrower from them, put his right arm into the harness, and Blue Jay helped him with the other. As Blue Jay fastened the front of the harness, Bean checked out the business end of the flamethrower.

While Bean was checking out the nozzle, Blue Jay inquired, "You do know how to use this thing, don't you?"

"No sweat," Bean answered. "In Special Forces, we used them at weenie roasts."

"Be careful you don't roast your own weenie," Blue Jay advised, then added, "Remember that fuel comes out of that nozzle under a lot of pressure, so don't forget to lean into it before you squeeze the trigger."

"Yes, Mother," Bean replied.

"Does this bring back any memories?" Benz asked Panda.

"You mean like Pakistan and the firefight at the warlord's compound?" he questioned.

"For starters," Benz replied.

"Don't pay any attention to them Mary-Margaret, you just go over there and smoke that puppy," Blue Jay instructed with a smile.

Having everything secured and ready to go, Bean approached the cave's entrance as the others prepared to move out. After taking up a position to fire, he leaned forward and only squeezed the back trigger with his right index finger that allowed fuel to pass through the nozzle and into the cave without igniting it. This allowed him to wet down the area before igniting it. Being satisfied, Bean let up on the trigger and the fuel stopped gushing out. He then took a more firm stance, squeezed the front trigger with his left index finger to light a match that would ignite the fuel, then he again squeezed the rear trigger and the fuel again gushed out of the nozzle, but this time, a steady stream of fire went into the cave sticking to and burning anything it touched. When the new flaming fuel touched the fuel already in the cave, an immediate inferno erupted. Seeing he had accomplished what he was trying to do, Bean eased up on both triggers, moved away from the cave, and started torching tents and everything else in the camp. When the fuel ran out, he was assisted in removing the flamethrower, put on his backpack, and Panda handed over the MP5 he was holding for him.

"I say, are you chaps having a weenie roast?" Pru inquired, referring to Bean's comment that came over the com earlier. "That force saw the smoke and have picked up their pace."

"We are preparing to move out," Blue Jay replied. "You know the plan; start moving to intercept us en route."

"Roger," was the one-word reply.

As flames engulfed the cave and most of the camp, the Team moved quickly along the shoreline on their way to their extraction point.

While still on the move, Blue Jay reached for the mike of the longer-range com unit he was carrying, pressed the button on the mike, and said, "Tea party went well. Uninvited guests trying to crash the party. See you soon."

CHAPTER FIFTEEN

The Board members on the yacht were getting a little anxious when there was no word from the Team, but were relieved when JJ appeared and informed them, "Everything went as planned and the Team is on their way out.

"Foxie is alerting the boats to move to the extraction point for pickup."

Everything was still quiet where the boats had landed. Still set up in their fan type defense, the six watched closely for any type of movement in their areas.

Top Kiner was scanning the area out in front of his position when Foxie came onto the com. "People returning from tea," were the only four words.

"Jolly good," was the two-word reply, then Top Kiner clicked the button on the mike of the other com unit three times and the other five knew it was time to leave.

First, the three furthest out rejoined the persons closest to the beach, then both returned to the beach and rejoined the others.

After a quick pause, the drivers ran to their boats, unsecured the moorings, jumped in, and started them. After all boats were ready to go, Jar Head, Doggie, and Swabbie stood and walked backward toward the boats scanning and moving their weapons from side-to-side as they went.

When they were almost at water's edge, Lady1 said, "These old farts *almost* look like they know what they are doing."

"I told you it was *almost* too early to send them to the home," LadyA replied.

"Can we make arrangements for other transportation?" Doggie inquired.

"No, I'm afraid we're stuck with these two peckernecks," Jar Head answered.

"Peckernecks," the Ladies said at the same time then burst into laughter.

"How bad," Top commented with a chuckle at the exchange, as the three men climbed into the boats and all departed to pick up the Team.

The Team was just off the beach as they quickly moved toward their extraction point. It probably wasn't the smartest route, but not knowing the exact size of the opposing force or where they all were, it seemed like a good choice, and unless a force popped out of the water, they couldn't be flanked from the right.

Staying off the beach, they left no tracks that could be easily spotted and they were out of immediate view. It wasn't easy running in the sand, but the Team always stayed in excellent condition and were up to the challenge.

————

The opposing force had reached the camp and as they were checking out the dead and what remained of the camp, their scouts looked for signs of what they now realized was the group the plan was created for in the first place.

"Things haven't worked out as originally planned, but the end result will be the same. We'll eradicate this group," the commander of the force confided to his subordinates.

When the Seal and the Major departed the camp, they took different routes and planned to meet again a short distance away.

When the Team departed, they covered their trail for only a short distance. They knew the trail would be picked up anyway and wanted to move at a fast pace to get some distance between themselves and the larger force.

It didn't take long for the scouts to report the tracks of a group moving up the shoreline. There were other individual tracks leaving the camp, but that was chalked up to normal activities or people fleeing the attack on the camp and was ignored.

When the commander got all of the reports from his scouts, he motioned for his radio man.

The two decoys had not gone unnoticed and men had been sent by the commander to check out the sightings.

The unit he sent to the site were the parachute jumpers went into the water could be moved into a position where they could intercept the group he was pursuing, catching them between the two forces.

The unit sent to check out the boats was a good distance away and it would probably take too much time to get them into position, but the commander would bring them into play anyway.

The commander got on the radio, told the unit leaders the situation, and ordered them to proceed along the shoreline to try to intercept the group they were trying to destroy.

The pickup for the Seal and the Major was simple and straightforward. A piper cub aircraft would land on the beach up the coast from the Al-Qaida camp, pick up the two passengers, and take off again. This was not an unusual activity for this island. Since it was uninhabited, visitors usually arrived by boat, but it was not unusual to see a small plane sitting on the beach.

Having arrived at the coordinates, the Seal was on the radio and had established communications with the plane Di Flippi had arranged for insertion and extraction of the two men.

As the two sat waiting for the plane, Major Tex said, "I wonder how big that force is that is after the others?"

"Was wondering that myself," the Seal replied.

As the two continued their discussion, the Al-Qaida sniper had the Major in his scope. He still had the container and was the primary objective.

The Al-Qaida sniper took a breath, let half of it out, started his trigger squeeze, then the sound of an AK Sniper Rifle firing broke the tranquil atmosphere.

I always said this AK sniper rifle was jolly good, The Brit thought to himself, as the Al-Qaida sniper tumbled from his concealed firing position. *Now I have to figure best way to make contact with these chaps.*

The Major and Seal had quickly taken up defensive positions. They heard the shot then caught a glimpse of a man tumbling forward and figured what had happened, but to who, by whom, was still a mystery.

Several minutes had passed when they both noticed someone walking on the beach heading in their direction and he was not wearing your normal beachwear. Unless you considered a camouflage ghillie suit and a rifle being carried at sling arms as normal.

As the man approached, the two watched his every move thinking it might be some sort of trap.

"Hello, chaps!" the man greeted the other two. "That sniper has been shadowing you since you left camp."

The two men didn't reply and The Brit said, "I see, not sure what I'm about. Well, let's see, I've worked with Blue Jay and Bean before."

When he saw the two men had a look of wonderment on their faces, he remarked, "Ho, dear, this is going to be difficult."

"Maybe not," the Seal offered, as he took the mike of his long-range com unit in hand and pressed the button. After Blue Jay came on, he explained the situation and for verification, the Seal was instructed to ask two questions. Place and year they had originally met and the place and year The Brit had suggested during their last meeting.

The answers verified it was The Brit, especially when he added during his reply, "Ho, I almost forgot, and the real answer is…"

"Glad we have that out of the way," The Brit admitted. He then explained he had a visit from Blue Jay and Bean. They asked questions about the island and that since he was a newsy bloke, decided to pop over to see what they were up to. Also, how he had seen them leave the camp, was followed by the sniper, and decided to tag along.

As he finished his story, the piper cub was landing on the beach in front of them.

As the three men stood up, The Brit said, "Cheero," as he started to walk away.

"Need a ride?" Major Tex inquired.

"No, thank you. Have my own plus I want to see how your chaps are getting on with that large force that is pursuing them."

"That's what we were wondering, too," the Major replied. He then asked, "Can your transportation handle additional passengers?"

"Good show," The Brit approved, as he motioned for them to join him.

After giving the container to the pilot of the plane and the Seal placing a call on the throwaway cell phone he was carrying, the two men, over the objections of Di, joined The Brit and all three quickly moved off the beach.

Being very familiar with the island and knowing where most of the players were located that day, The Brit set a direct course for where he calculated the larger force would probably be.

CHAPTER SIXTEEN

When the speedboats arrived at the extraction point, they were gently beached like before, but this time, the six were not a decoy and had set up in a defensive position that included both directions on the beach.

One hour had passed since their arrival when Top Kiner motioned to everyone they might have company at the right front of their position and everyone silently clicked off the safeties on their weapons.

Top was right, they did have company. It was a scout from one of the units moving to intercept the Team.

The scout reported back to the unit leader who then got on the radio to the force commander. "Sir, one of my scouts has discovered what looked like three high speedboats on the beach and at least six people in position just off the beach. Should I engage them?"

The commander quickly analyzed the new information and concluded the boats were the way the group he was pursuing planned to leave the island. If he told his men to bypass the boats, some of this group may get away when they were engaged, make it to the boats, and escape. If the six were killed and with the boats in the hands of his men, the group would have no way to leave the island.

Wanting to destroy the entire group and knowing his unit outnumbered the others three to one, he ordered, "Engage the six and take control of the boats."

"Yes, sir," the unit leader replied, then set about the business of planning the attack on the six.

The force commander's reasoning would have been sound if he were not dealing with these people.

Truth be told, he would probably have a better chance at sticking a wet noodle up a wild cat's ass than defeating these six with a force of that size.

"Back with friends," Top whispered into the com, as he raised his favorite weapon—the M14—and prepared to fire. LadyA and Lady1 did the same with their M1 carbines, as the other three readied their MP5s.

The six didn't have to wait long. The leader had decided the majority of his force would perform a frontal attack and after the assault got underway, five of his men would assault the position on their left flank.

The six could hear the unit moving in then a whistle blew and all hell broke loose. The six stayed low for the initial rapid rate of fire that comes from the enemy when the attack is started.

"Doesn't anybody practice fire control anymore?" Jar Head questioned Top Kiner who just smiled and shrugged his shoulders.

When the initial rate of fire subsided, the six responded with deadly fire into the ranks of the attacking force, but there were a lot of them and they kept coming.

"Left flank!" Lady1 yelled, as she and LadyA engaged the attacking force. As one then two came into view, the Ladies quickly dispatched them. When three more appeared, they switched the selectors on their weapons to full automatic and both fired into the oncoming three taking them out.

Top was performing at his usual rate, one shot, one down, as he quickly worked his way across the attackers' front row.

Swabbie, Jar Head, and Doggie kept up a study stream of automatic weapons fire going at the frontal assault. When Doggie and Jar Head were reloading, Swabbie filled in the void.

The fire from the six had brought the advance to a halt, but the force didn't retreat, they just found cover and returned fire.

"Fuck this," Doggie said to Jar Head during their second reload.

"I agree," Jar Head replied.

The Team heard the firefight when it started, were concerned their people at the boats were under fire, and picked up their pace.

"Maybe it's a unit from that big force in a firefight with some Al-Qaida types?" Bean said into the com. But before Blue Jay could respond, the sound of two explosions could be heard.

"Now what do you think?" Blue Jay inquired.

"It's the boats," Bean acknowledged. "I think Jar Head and Doggie definitely have a thing about those fucking fragmentation grenades."

"Maybe the frags fill a void left from never having a pet when they were children?" Blue Jay offered.

After the two explosions, all gunfire subsided. "Sounds like they got somebody's attention," Bean observed.

"That force behind us has split into two groups and it looks like the smaller lead group is pulling away from the others," Benz advised and everyone came to a halt.

"Sending their better unit on ahead," Bean observed.

"There goes our window for getting to the boats and shoving off before that big force arrived," Blue Jay said into the com then inquired, "What are you doing?" as he observed Bean removing his backpack.

"Going to slow that advanced unit down a little to make sure we can hook up with our people at the pickup point," he replied, as he removed an old fragmentation grenade from this pack. "Doggie gave me this grenade back in the early nineties. Do you still carry the one Jar Head gave you?"

"Yeah, but hold up a second. Let's talk about this," Blue Jay instructed.

"I figure fifteen on our side is better than nine when we go up against that bigger force, but if these eager beavers force us into a firefight along the way…" Bean stopped his sentence knowing everyone knew what he was going to say.

"What's your plan?" Blue Jay inquired.

"Just a quick stealthy delaying tactic to make them more cautious and slow them down a little," he replied.

"Okay," Blue Jay agreed, as he removed his backpack to retrieve the grenade. "But no heroics."

"I'll drop back and rig the grenades up with trip wires. After they run across them, they should advance with a little more caution," Bean advised.

Blue Jay gave Bean the grenade as the Team helped him add more foliage to his ghillie suit, so he could better blend into his surroundings.

When Bean was ready, Blue Jay said, "Let's move out," into the com and everyone wished Bean luck as they left the area.

Blue Jay was the last to leave and instructed, "Now don't piss me off because you got yourself killed."

"I'll try not to," Bean replied. "Wouldn't want to leave you alone to deal with our fathers."

"I didn't think of that," Blue Jay replied. "On second thought, maybe I'll stay with you."

Both men smiled and after wishing him luck, Blue Jay left to catch up with the others, as Bean moved back in the direction of the pursuing force.

After traveling a very short distance, Bean found a location he liked and set up a wire at ankle height where he thought someone in the quick moving force would trip it setting off the grenades.

Having secured the grenades to separate trees, he connected them using a wire that was secured to the pull rings of each grenade. After making sure the wire was reasonably taut, he straightened out the cotter pins that secured the pull rings to the grenade a little, making sure the pins didn't slide all the way out and detonate the grenade prematurely.

When this task was done, he moved off in the direction the Team had taken and melted into the landscape a good distance away.

"What's your status," Foxie inquired on the com.

While still on the move, Blue Jay pushed the mike on the longer-range com. "Left the dance, but am being followed by a group that is mad we departed."

"Are you close to your ride home?" Foxie asked.

"Yes, will play it by ear from then on."

The lead unit of the big force was quickly approaching the trip wires as Bean watched intensely from his concealed position. The first man missed the wire and since they were traveling almost in single file, the others would probably miss it as well.

So much for a stealthy delay tactic, Bean thought to himself, as he raised the MP5 and fired on the lead man knowing the others would scatter.

When the lead man went down, the others went for cover and one of them hit the trip wire, the cotter pins were pulled out, the spoons clicked, and within seconds, two explosions erupted.

This was not the desired result. The grenades were supposed to go off when the opposing force were on their feet, not lying down.

After the two explosions, Bean started moving out of the area, but was spotted by the leader of the unit, and he directed his men to fire in Bean's area.

As rounds started impacting in Bean's surroundings, he thought, *These guys are special forces types. Probably trained in the U.S., too.*

Knowing his position had been compromised, Bean moved faster and occasionally returned fire to keep his pursuers' honest.

Doggie and Jar Head's frags seemed to convince the attacking unit to back off and they were in full retreat.

The Team was now within com range and everyone could hear Blue Jay inquire, "Anybody on?"

Before anyone else could reply, Lady1 inquired, "Is that you F troop? Late again."

"And yet again, our concerns have been misplaced," Blue Jay replied, as the Team chuckled at the question and answer. "Our ETA is about ten minutes and we have brought a few for tea," Blue Jay alerted the six. "We won't have time to get underway, so we'll have to make a stand."

"We'll set up a perimeter defense and you people can fill in the gaps when you arrive," Top Kiner advised.

"Sounds good," he replied.

The perimeter defense was set up with the boat drivers at the ends closest to the beach and the other three forming the perimeter curve.

The Team arrived and immediately filled in the empty spaces in the perimeter defense. Pru and Met set up their M82s facing in the direction of the oncoming force with Top Kiner and his M14 right alongside them. The .417 rounds would reach way out there and whittle down the attackers. Top would engage them when they got into the five-yard range.

Not like hearing all of that gunfire so soon after the two explosions, Blue Jay announced, "Be careful. The turd in the lead may be one of ours," then he brought the six up to date about the force that was about to arrive and the larger force behind it.

"I say, there was a chap running in the open, but now has changed direction and is heading toward the wooded area," Pru said into the com, as he looked through the scope mounted on his M82 rifle.

Blue Jay asked Benz for the use of his spotter scope and after looking through it for a few seconds, announced, "Yeah, that's Mr. Stealth himself. I didn't eat my gypsy shit this morning, but I'd say he wants you to take out anybody that tries to follow him."

He was still talking when the M82's started firing at the force in pursuit.

"Now that was just a guess," Blue Jay continued. "I hope Mr. Stealth wasn't the second man."

"Quite," Pru replied, knowing Bean was the first man.

The M82s were taking their toll, but the force was serving its purpose.

When the commander of that force sent them on ahead, he probably pumped their heads full of bullshit, but all he was really using them for was a delaying tactic.

The .417 rounds slowed their progress, but they kept coming then Top's M14 started barking. The leader finally ordered the force into an area where the trees were more plentiful. It became harder to hit their targets and the outgoing rate of fire slowed down considerably.

When Bean rejoined the others, he saw what type of defense they were in and took a position in the parameter.

"Did someone just join us?" Blue Jay inquired to the others. "If someone did, they really know how to be stealthy."

"Get stuffed," Bean replied.

"Is that you, Bean?" Blue Jay said with fake surprise. "You are getting just too good at this stealth shit."

Bean made a quick reply and the duo were again in a verbal skirmish.

———————

When the main force arrived, they were informed about the long-range snipers and all joined the lead group in the more wooded area.

"Well, that's good and bad," Doggie observed. "It makes it harder to hit them at long range, but at least we have a good idea about where they will be attacking from."

"Are you from this planet?" Bean inquired. "Did your parents have any children that actually lived?"

"I'm shocked and amazed at these questions," Doggie said with fake surprise.

"How many times did I say you were spoiling the lad when we had him in training?" Jar Head reprimanded.

"Like yours is any better," Doggie replied.

"Why, I'm proud of Blue Jay and what he has become," Jar
Head defended.

"Don't you old fucks get me into it," Blue Jay advised.

"You're right, Doggie, neither one of them are worth a shit," Jar Head announced.

The Team always enjoyed these little exchanges. If a person didn't know better, it seemed like they didn't care for each other, but the extreme opposite was true. The four had put their lives on the line for each other more than once in the past and would be willing to do it again in the future.

CHAPTER SEVENTEEN

The force commander was planning his attack and after the two unit leaders gave their reports, he knew these people had to be taken very seriously, regardless of the odds.

Using the beach to assault their position would be too costly. He had big odds in his favor, wanted to keep it that way and finally decided on a frontal assault. That was both a good and bad decision. It put many people on line for the assault, but bunched them into a small area creating several rows that allowed only the front row to fire freely.

———

Blue Jay's plan for defense was simple. Since he had no light or heavy machine guns, he would build around the M82s. No long-range shooting this time, but they would cause a lot of intimidation as those big ass rounds passed through the ranks of the attacking force.

Each M82's field of fire would be half of the parameter front and would overlap with the other M82. Everyone else was assigned an individual field of fire that overlapped with the person to the left and right of them. Everyone knew how fire control worked, so ammunition shouldn't be a problem, for a while anyway.

The frags would come in handy and were being distributed. When Jar Head got to LadyA, he started to hand her a grenade, then pulled it back. "I forgot; you throw like a girl."

"Well, you gave one to him didn't you?" she replied, pointing at Bean.

Bean just smile and flipped her the bird and got one in return.

"Well, I'll give you one, but don't waste it," Jar Head instructed and was also flipped the bird.

He then moved onto Lady1, but before he could say anything, she said, "Just give me one, you old fart."

"Another friend made," Doggie observed.

"And it only took one boat ride," LadyA added.

"Now you see the shit we have to put up with?" Blue Jay chimed in.

"All right, children, but remember what they say about paybacks," Jar Head said with a smile.

The four looked at each other and chuckled, as Jar Head returned to his defensive position.

With grenades distributed and interlinking fields of fire assigned, the defenders waited for the attack.

The force commander had instructed his troops and they were moving into position. Once they got on line, the signal was given to advance and they all started moving forward.

Bris who had been set up out in front of their position returned and informed Blue Jay about the advancing troops, then took his place in the parameter defense.

Now knowing the attacking force was bunched up, Blue Jay said, "Let's start this dance," and instructed Pru and Met to start firing at a slow rate. The objective was not so much to hit, but rather to intimidate the force.

Only a few of the .417 rounds found their marks, but that's all it took. The other men saw what damage that round could do and the pace slowed down considerably.

It took longer than expected, but the force finally got to their jumping off point and the defense braced for the initial attack.

Whistles blew, men started shooting and charging their position.

The defenders used the same tactic as before. Wait until after the initial firing of the attack, and then come up firing.

"Let's do it," Blue Jay instructed and 15 weapons opened fire.

Only firing within their assigned interlocking fields of fire, the defenders took a serious toll on the first row of the attackers, but they weren't discouraged and kept advancing.

"Shit going out!" Doggie yelled and everyone ducked down. The telltale sounds of the spoons flying off hand grenades were heard, as they went in the enemy's direction. After two explosions shook the ground, everyone again came up firing and the first assault on their position was beaten back.

The force regrouped, discussed the strategy used by the defenders, moved more of their automatic weapons to the front, and were again assaulting the position.

This time, when the defenders rose up, a hail of bullets would meet them.

The attackers again started with a large volume of fire, but as it subsided, the defenders didn't pop up. Instead, the sounds of seven spoons flying off hand grenades could be heard followed by seven explosions. The defenders came up firing and the attack never really got started.

As they retreated, Blue Jay was on the com. "I don't know why this turd isn't hitting our flanks, but I'm sure that's going to change. Let's do an ammo check."

The M82s were running low, but Pru and Met still had their MP5s. The others were also starting to run low, but had their sidearms with a few extra magazines before they would be totally out. A few grenades were also left. Check and Tic reported they each had a few high explosive rounds for their M79 grenade launchers and figured they would save them for the grand finale or the next attack, whichever came first.

"Use the remaining grenades against any flanking movements that may occur," Blue Jay instructed, as he and the others unsnapped the straps that kept their sidearms from falling out of their holsters.

This time, the attacking force did not start with a heavy volume of fire, but tried to get as close as possible before firing and were also executing flanking movements from the left and right.

"Tic, Check," Blue Jay said into the com and pointed to the front of the parameter. Seconds later, the pong sounds of two HE rounds going out were heard quickly followed by two more. The explosions slowed down the frontal assault, but the flanking movements picked up speed.

One of the flanking movements were quickly advancing on LadyA and Lady1's positions, as they pulled the pins on two grenades. "Shit going out," LadyA advised into the com and a few seconds later, telltale ping sounds of two spoons flying off grenades were heard followed by two ground shaking explosions.

"Let's do it," Blue Jay said into the com and the defenders came up firing. and the dance was on.

Hearing the pinging sounds of spoons flying off of grenades, a few in the rear of the flanking unit dropped to the ground and weren't that affected by the blasts and came up firing.

LadyA and Lady1 returned fire, but these few must have been high on something because the high velocity rounds from the M1 carbines passing through their bodies didn't seem to slow them down.

Noticing that fact, the Ladies changed to headshots and finally stopped them when they were very close to their position.Top Kiner was firing to the front and at the same time keeping an eye on his right flank.

Top was in the process of removing an empty magazine from his M-14 when three men of the attacking force thought they saw an opportunity and charged.

Top saw the attackers and announced, "On the right flank," as he quickly drew his pistol and three shots later, three men were falling to the ground.

After they had stopped the last few attackers on their flank, Lady1 and LadyA quickly turned to check the right flank just in time to see Top down the three men.

"I've said it before and I'll say it again, I have always liked Top's cooking," LadyA admitted, as they turned their attention back to the left flank.

"Best I've ever had," Lady1 agreed. "Wouldn't want him to get the idea we didn't like it."

"Exactly," LadyA confirmed.

"How bad?" Top said after hearing the comments over the com as he rejoined the firefight.

The Team was running low on ammo and had started to share when Foxie's voice came on the long-range com. "What's your status?"

"In a firefight just off the beach, can't get to the boats, and running low on ammo," Blue Jay reported.

"Well that's not good," Foxie replied. "Throw some smoke between your position and the attackers, count to sixty, then run for the boats," he suggested.

Blue Jay removed a smoke grenade attached to his web gear, pulled the pin, threw it to the front of their position and started to count.

The firefight was hitting a fever pitch as red smoke filled the air when a helicopter flew over their position and fire from three automatic weapons spewed out of the opened side door of the chopper spraying the attackers and was accompanied by an explosion that erupted in the middle of the enemy force.

A second chopper quickly followed with another three automatic weapons firing out their side door.

JC, Jockey, and the Board made up what everyone referred to during planning as, 'The poor man's air support.'

Three men lying in the prone position with the barrels of their weapons pointing out the door would fire on command until the magazines of their MP5's were empty, unless you were Wilson who insisted on using his Sub Thomson machine gun.

Mac, in the first chopper, would fire a single shot grenade launcher and keep an eye on Weed Whacker's fire control.

By the time Jockey had made his first pass, JC had already made a quick reverse turn and was starting his second. "Pull pins and prepare to throw," Mac instructed and they all pulled the pins on four smoke grenades.

"Now remember, it's going to be by the numbers," Mac instructed. "Wilson, are you one?"

"No, I'm not. Are you one?"

"Oh, that's cute," Mac said, shaking his head.

As the chopper passed over the enemy force, JC counted over the com, "One, two, three, four," and on each count, a smoke grenade was dropped and fell to the ground between the opposing forces.

Jockey had also made a quick reverse turn, but his return trip was directly over the enemy force and the people in his ship dropped gas grenades using the same method.

Not wanting to set up a pattern, JC held position after his second pass, dropped down below the tree line, and out of sight until the other ship had made its second pass.

"Weed Whacker, try to hit something besides foliage next time," Mac instructed.

"Get knotted," Wilson replied, as he attached a full drum of ammo to his Sub Thompson.

"Pass completed," Jockey alerted over the radio and JC raised the ship up above the tree line. "Do it," he said into the com and again, weapons fire came out of the opened door.

Blue Jay counted 60 then ordered, "To the boats," into the com and the defenders started moving across the beach. Lady1, LadyA, and Top ran to their boats, jumped in, and got the powerful engines of the three boats fired up and ready to go.

The others made a tactical withdraw incase anyone came charging through the dense smoke that separated them from the attacking force. When everyone arrived at the boats, they unsecured the mooring lines, pushed them off the sand, and boarded the crafts.

Jockey had taken up a position just off the beach and was joined shortly by JC. The two helicopters kept changing their positions and continued firing on the enemy force through the smoke while the three boats got underway. When they were about 100 yards offshore and traveling at full speed, the two helicopters broke off their engagement with the enemy force and departed taking separate routes, but in the same direction as the boats.

The Brit, Seal, and Major Tex had arrived just in time to see the three boats speed out to sea and decided to move onto The Brit's plane before this force regrouped and conducted a search of the area for anyone who may have been left behind.

Moving quickly, they were out of the immediate area and heading back toward the coastline before heading for the location where the plane was parked.

Unbeknownst to them, the unit sent to check out the boat report had the same idea about traveling along the coast and were approaching at a 45-degree angle from the opposite direction.

When the three arrived at the beach they cautiously approached, then checked for anyone on the beach. The Brit and Seal first looked to the right while the Major scanned to the left.

As his line of sight approached the tree line to the left, an armed man appeared, started to raise his weapon, but was cut down by a quick burst from an MP5. "Told you I was quick," the Major said to the Seal just before the area behind the man erupted and rounds started whizzing past the three men.

After the three dove for cover, The Brit said, "A bit of activity seems to have come our way."

"Looks more like a bunch of activity," Major Tex replied.

While stopping to reload, the Major looked over at the Seal who was on the radio. "Calling home," he explained.

"Say hi to Mom for me," the Major requested, then fired another short burst at the larger force.

The firefight continued with the opposing force unable to get the upper hand.

The Major had again dropped down to reload shortly followed by the others when two eager beavers on the opposing force stood up and charged their position. The Major saw the move, drew his sidearm, and fired two well-aimed rounds dropping the two men in their tracks. The Seal looked at him and Major Tex said, "When they get

Surgeons of Terror 5 – Yar Island

hit by the 1911, they stay hit." He was referring to the model 1911 .45 caliber semiautomatic pistol he was carrying.

"It does seem that way," The Brit observed.

The firing subsided for a while and the three knew the opposing force had given up or they were planning something.

Suddenly, a large volume of fire came from the opposing force shortly followed by four men assaulting their position from the left flank. The Seal fired a burst from his MP5 taking down two of them from a kneeling position then dove, rolled, and fired again taking down the other two.

Seeing he was all right, The Brit commented to the Major, "A bit acrobatic wouldn't you say?"

"Quite," Major Tex agreed.

The Seal shook his head and smiled at their comments, as he crawled back to his original position.

Knowing the GPS coordinates of the three men, the two ships raced up the coastline and it didn't take long to arrive onsite.

Since there was no way for the helicopters to know the exact locations of the bad guys, they hovered just off the beach. The Seal acted as Forward Observer and directed them into position before they started firing.

With all of that additional incoming fire, the opposing force broke and ran. The ships stopped firing and the three very quickly moved onto where the plane was parked.

The helicopters moved several hundred yards offshore and escorted the three to The Brit's plane.

2157

After saying thanks over the com and waving to the ships, the three were in the plane and underway.

After the plane was airborne and a safe distance away, the ships turned and headed out to sea to rejoin the three boats.

CHAPTER EIGHTEEN

As the two helicopters approached the speeding boats from behind, JC was on the radio to Jockey. "If I didn't know better, I'd say we have a race back to home base in progress."

"Well, let me see," Jockey pondered. "Tic and Check used to race these types of boats. During the planning stage, they somehow managed to get themselves assigned to separate boats and Lady1 is driving the other one. I'd say they were racing."

"Can't leave these children unsupervised for ten minutes," JC jokingly complained.

The two ships reduced speed and swung to the left or right and both ran parallel with speeding crafts.

The Board members were lying on the floors of the helicopters looking up and thinking about the day's activities and were happy they had survived it all when JC's voice came on the com. "Any of you people want to watch a boat race?"

The Board members on both ships looked at each other then looked out of the opened doorways.

After watching for a while, Dawson inquired, "Anyone want to place a bet?"

"If memory serves, two of those people down there have a lot of experience racing. What boat are they in?" Howard inquired.

Mac was watching the race through his field glasses and answered, "Tic and Check are in separate boats, not at the wheel, but are standing right next to the drivers. Lady1 is driving the third boat with Jar Head, Bean, Benz, and Panda onboard. I'd say we have all kinds of racing going on down there. House Team against each other, Tic against Check, Blue Jay against Bean. Jar Head, Doggie, and Swabbie in separate boats. My opinion, two of the boats have expert advisors onboard and that should give them the edge, but that fact will just make the third boat more competitive and determined to win."

For betting purposes, it was decided to identify the racers as

Tic, Check, and The Determined Ones.

"I'll bet a thousand on Tic," Howard announced.

"You're covered," Dawson replied.

"A thousand on Check," Dunn announced.

"You got it," Wilson informed him.

That was a little steep for Jockey, Foxie, JC, and Mac, so they decided to pull their money and placed a bet on The Determined Ones.

JJ felt funny about betting against any of the racers, so he bet a thousand on each boat with all winnings going to a worthy cause. The other Board members agreed and covered his bet.

It was an exciting race. The Check and Tic boats were neck and neck with The Determined Ones almost even with them. The motors on all three boats were screaming, but Top, LadyA, and Lady1 kept the pedal to the metal as the boats skimmed across the water.

The Determined Ones didn't know that much about racing, but reasoned Tic and Check wouldn't push their boats too hard, so they decided to just keep pace until the finish line was in sight.

The Board members were enjoying the race when all of the sudden, Wilson started laughing for no apparent reason. The other three in the helicopter looked at him and he explained over the com, "I was just thinking. Seven years ago, I was busy running a company with only retirement to look forward to, then JJ called. We have been getting involved more and more in the operational side of the Projects and today, we were engaged in two firefights immediately followed by a day at the boat races," and started laughing again.

"Makes one wonder doesn't it?" Howard remarked, as the entire Board burst into laughter.

The boats and helicopters were all heading for two small islands known as Tortuguillos about 20 miles to the west of Tortuga.

It was decided during the planning stage that Tortuguillos would be used as home base for the operation. To reduce the chance of discovery, time at the two very small islands would be held to a minimum.

Since it was not unusual for very wealthy people on very expensive rented or owned crafts to sail in these waters, a yacht would be used as a cover. The original plan was to use a yacht the Board was forced to purchase after a previous Project, but time would not allow transporting it to this area from a marina on the west coast of Mexico. It was finally decided a yacht would be rented with the Board hoping it wouldn't be shot up like the last one.

A cover was just one of the functions the yacht performed.

With the drivers at the wheels, the three speedboats would be towed in single file to Tortuguillos with dawn being their ETA.

The yacht would also carry barrels of fuel for the helicopters and speedboats. After their long flight from Bonaire, the helicopters would definitely require refueling prior to them taking up station off the coast of Tortuga in case the Teams required air support.

Using a makeshift pulley system JC, Mac, and Jockey had developed, Mac would assemble it on the yacht and use it to load the barrels onto temporary platforms on each of the three speedboats.

Each boat would ferry one barrel at a time the short distance to the island and push them off the platform at the edge of the beach, so they could be rolled to two separate landing positions.

When that was completed, they would shove off for Tortuga and their first stop on the island.

They had hit a few snags along the way like the pulley system and the helicopters arriving later than expected, but with everyone contributing a 110 percent, everything went off as planned.

———————

Blue Jay was in communication with JC and asked if the two choppers would act as judges at the finish line.

As JC and Jockey increased speed, they informed the others, "We have been asked to declare the winner with the yacht being the finish line."

"Holy shit, I hope we aren't going to buy another yacht," Dunn said into the com.

"Don't worry," Howard advised him. "How could they not see and hit something that big?"

"Are we talking about the same people?" Dunn inquired.

"They are running side-by-side and a craft at anchor tends to move around the anchor chain," Foxie informed them over the com.

"Thank you for those encouraging remarks, Admiral Fox," Wilson said in a loud voice.

"Just an observation," Foxie said, as he shrugged his shoulders.

"Tell Weed Whacker we'll chip in our pooled bet money to help pay for the yacht," Mac said into the com.

"Yeah, we'll chip in our pooled bet money to help pay for the yacht," Foxie echoed Mac's remark.

"And we really don't want to hear any shit out of you, Talley Whacker," Wilson replied, as Mac and Foxie chuckled.

The helicopters were set up on the finish line as all three boats were at full throttle, as they approached the finish line.

"Seriously, folks," Foxie again spoke into the com. "Those boats are running so close it's not allowing them any wiggle room."

"Maybe we should tell them to back off," JJ said.

"Are we talking about the same people?" Dunn again asked.

"Yeah, what was I thinking?" JJ confessed with a smile.

As the speedboats approached the yacht, it was swinging at anchor as Foxie had told them and it looked like the boats would pass very close to it, but no one was changing course.

"The boat on the far left might want to think about backing off," Foxie advised.

"Who did you say was driving that boat?" Dawson inquired.

"Lady1," Mac informed him.

"We're fucked!" Wilson exclaimed. "There goes another yacht."

The three boats were evenly matched with no one being able to get the advantage. Tic and Check had the skills, but as the name implied, the other boat had a lot of determination.

"Am I the only one that has noticed that big assed yacht up ahead?" Jar Head inquired.

"What yacht?" Lady1 answered, keeping totally focused on the race.

"That's what I thought," Jar Head answered, as he and Bean exchanged smiles then shook their heads.

The yacht seemed to be swinging a little faster as the boats bared down on the finish line.

Lady1 had excellent perception, but that puppy was moving into her path a little quicker than she would have liked; but that didn't matter.

As the three boats approached the yacht, a collision looked inevitable, and JC was on the radio. "Jockey, in case we have a collision, how do you want to work this?"

"I'm a little closer, so I'll hover at water level around the number three boat."

"I'll wait to make sure the other two are all right before I join you," JC confirmed.

"Roger," Jockey acknowledged.

The boats were about 50 yards from the yacht when Check instructed over the com, "Passengers on all boats move to the right side of the crafts."

"Now, people!" Tic affirmed the instruction and everyone moved quickly as instructed.

At these speeds, 50 yards are covered in no time at all and within seconds, the three boats were on top of the yacht that was swinging into their paths.

"What just happened?" Howard inquired with a look of disbelief on his face.

"I've seen a lot of close ones before, but not that close," Foxie admitted.

All three boats had made it past the yacht in a dead heat.

The Determined Ones by a coat of paint and the race was declared a tie.

"The next time, we have to look into contracting A1 Speed Boat Drivers," Dunn commented.

"Well, it looks like we lucked out again, Foxie," Mac informed his old friend. "Their for a second thought, you and I would be contributing two hundred and fifty dollars each toward a new yacht."

Wilson just looked at Mac who inquired, "What?" with faked innocence.

"Would someone please pass me that Sub Thompson?" Wilson asked, pointing to the weapon.

"So you actually did see the yacht?" Jar Head inquired.

"What yacht?" Lady1 again questioned, as the boat slowed and she guided it toward the beach.

"Ho, that's funny," Jar Head replied, "almost as funny as the first time you said it."

As the three boats approached the beach, the two ships were landing and there was no time to waste.

The helicopter's fuel had to be topped off before they started their long flight back and the speedboats also had to be refueled then gotten underway.

The plan was to get the helicopters and speedboats into international waters as soon as possible.

JC and Jockey would make the long return flight to Bonaire.

The yacht would leave at the same time as the others, rendezvous with the speedboats, and again set up a tow for the trip back.

With the barrels of fuel unloaded and the pulley system dismantled, if the yacht were stopped and boarded, it would just reveal seven wealthy men on a rented yacht sailing around the islands.

The yacht had rendezvoused with the speedboats, set up the tow, and were again underway.

JJ and Mac were standing at the back of the yacht smoking cigars and watching the speedboats that were in tow.

"We were again extremely fortunate," JJ said to his lifelong friend.

"Yes, we were," Mac agreed. "The planning was good, but people have to make plans work and our people get it done."

"I think with a group of lesser quality, it wouldn't have come off at all," JJ revealed.

"I agree," Mac confirmed.

The two continued smoking and didn't say anything for a while then Mac said, "There was one thing I wanted to accomplish while we were in the area, but we can only do so much."

"What was that?" JJ questioned with a puzzled look.

"Know you are concerned about the cost of such things, but I had hoped to contact the Tortuga freedom fighters and give them some of our weapons, maybe those M82s for starters," Mac said.

"There you go again, but I'm not going to lose it this time," JJ informed him.

"I don't understand?" Mac said with a look of innocence. "I thought you were in favor of groups that were fighting evil?"

"Know I'm going to regret continuing this conservation, but you know that Tortuga is a deserted island," JJ replied.

"Is it really?" Mac said with surprise. "I was planning on getting Tuna and Sunny Sands to bring over the weapons we gave them on previous Projects and join the fight."

"That would have been nice." JJ maintained his cool.

Mac was surprised the conversation had gone on this long, so he added, "Deserted island, how about that. Well, there is supposed to be buried treasure on Tortuga, so maybe we should go back, bury all the weapons, and draw a map incase any freedom fighters do show up sometime in the future?"

"I'll give you a fucking map," JJ finally lost it, as he again got Mac in a headlock due to the topic of conversation.

"Now we know the Project is definitely completed," Bean said to the Team and pointed at the two.

"That must have been a hard sell, especially since we still have all of the weapons," Bris observed.

"You know Mac," Panda said. "It probably went something like, *I want to mail the weapons to Tommy Tortuga, a guy that said he'd like to organize freedom fighters to fight the local government on the deserted island.*"

Between the headlock and Panda's narrative of what probably happened, the Team wound down a little as they all burst into laughter.

CHAPTER NINETEEN

Everyone had made a safe return to home base in New Jersey.

JJ was thankful and felt great relief they had taken no casualties, especially with all of their people involved in those firefights on Tortuga.

They even made out well in the equipment department. They still had the speedboats, helicopters, all the weapons, and they didn't even have to buy another yacht. Although toward the end of the boat race, Wilson had suggested that if it didn't sink, they name the yacht they were about to buy Big Cheese II after the first one.

From time to time, a big dinner party was held after the completion of a Project and JJ decided it was time to have another.

Top, LadyA, and Lady1 assisted by JJ and Mac always took care of the food and beverage part while the Team handled setting up the dining area, the security, and transportation of the Board members to and from the Barn.

Everyone was looking forward to it and even Di Flippi was making time to attend.

It was never given an official name and in the beginning was referred to as The After Project Dinner, but later became known as The Bull Shit Derby Dinner.

Everyone took their time with the planning and preparations, usually taking a week to complete.

———————

Blue Jay had excused himself for the day to tend to some personal business. After being on the road for about five hours, he turned onto a dirt road 10 miles northwest of Leesburg, Virginia. The road made its way through the forest and ended on the bank of the Potomac River in an area where both fisherman and people with pleasure crafts launch the boats into the river.

After parking in a designated area, Blue Jay got out of his car and took on the appearance of a hiker as he slung on a small backpack and started to walk along the Potomac while checking out the area for both friend and foe.

Several miles upriver, Blue Jay stopped and surveyed the entire area then disappeared into the woods. After making a wide sweep to make sure the area was secure, he returned to the river, but remained in the wooded area and out of sight.

As he waited, his thoughts wandered back to Jamaica and his encounter with Crazy when a voice inquired, "Is this where George Washington threw the silver dollar across the Potomac?"

Blue Jay was in deep thought and was a little startled by the voice, but quickly regained his composure. "No, I don't think so."

"I'm sorry, didn't mean to frighten you," a man apologized, as he appeared from the wooded area. "Next time I'll try to make more noise."

"If you make any more noise the next time, you may as well carry a flag and make it an official parade," Blue Jay advised.

"I saw you jump," the man replied.

"Just pretending," Blue Jay answered.

"Really? Well, we'll have to see about that won't we?" the man suggested.

"You rang?" Blue Jay asked, referring to the call he had received.

"Yes, I did," the man replied. "Someone is interfering with my livelihood and I want your opinion about something. Last year, I was retained about two very personal matters and after much planning, was in Cuba waiting for the right opportunity to eliminate both at the same time, but the opportunity never presented, so I decided to go ahead and eliminate one."

"Was in a remote area of Cuba where the Cuban VP was meeting with Raul when a small unit forced me to rush my shot. Now wait a minute, I think you were with that unit," Blue Jay's brother said mockingly.

"Maybe," was the noncommittal reply.

"Well, anyway," his brother continued, "as I said, there were two matters to be resolved and the second one is big in South America. This time, somebody raised so much hell on the island of Tortuga that the South America matter seems to have gone into hiding for some reason. Know of any reason why he would do that?"

"It's all news to me," Blue Jay confessed.

"Well, I know you get around and if you run across anyone that you feel may be interested in this information, tell them I'm very patient and the matter will be taken care of if no one scares him into hiding again."

"I'll keep my ears open," Blue Jay promised.

With the reason they met out of the way and since the two rarely got the chance to see each other, they continued their conversation talking about family and personal matters.

Some time had passed, as they walked along the banks of the Potomac when Blue Jay's brother inquired, "So, you think I made a lot of noise coming through the area?"

"Almost like a parade," Blue Jay answered, knowing that was not the truth. In fact, his brother was almost as good as he was when it came to moving quietly.

"Is that right?" he replied. "Well, that sounds like a challenge to me, so I'll practice up real hard and maybe give you a big surprise when and where you least expect it."

"Don't forget the flag," Blue Jay advised.

———

The Board was in session conducting their post-Project meeting and Mac had the floor. "I'd like to commend you people for doing a good job on the Project," he started. "I know you all had served in the military and a lot of years had passed since then, but you all performed well above expectations. Wouldn't you say, Admiral Fox?"

"Yes," he agreed then added, "For old fucks."

The Board was feeling good about Mac's words, but was snapped out of it by Foxie's remark, especially since it was way out of the norm for him to say anything like that.

Mac was not expecting the remark and was initially surprised, but then started laughing.

"You Navy peckerhead," Wilson yelled at Foxie who was now also laughing.

"You two cooked that up didn't you?" Dawson accused them and while Mac tried to claim innocence, Foxie was telling everyone it was all Mac's idea.

JJ and Dunn saw that the statement had surprised Mac, so they just sat back and enjoyed the melee.

Some time later, when everything finally got back to normal, JJ called the meeting back to order. They completed the post-Project meeting and had decided to discuss possible future Projects.

"Personally, I think we have a Project that is long overdue," JJ started. "It may be too ambitious, but if it is, we will find that out during our normal evaluation processes.

"Due to involvement in previous Projects, the target has already been assigned a codename. I'm sure you all remember Big Face."

CHAPTER TWENTY

T he Bullshit Derby Dinner went off as scheduled. After enjoying another excellent dinner,
everyone was having a coffee or an after dinner
drink and enjoying each other's company.

Since Foxie was instrumental in originally re-
cruiting the Seal for an earlier Project, he always
inquired about him when given the opportunity.
"Di, how is the Seal faring these days?"

"Funny you should ask," Di Flippi replied,
"Can't seem to get him back from the British Virgin Islands. First claimed he got bat fever from
that cave I made him go into and that he was laid
up. After a few more of those types of calls, did
some checking and found out the Seal, Major Tex,
and The Brit are in party hardy mode, raising hell
every night and even made a trip to Jamaica."

"Oh, shit," Bean said, knowing The Brit had
been stationed there for years.

"Exactly," Di confirmed. "After much threatening, thought I was making progress when he

told me the Major had bat fever and he didn't want to leave him stranded. When I suggested The Brit could watch out for him, he told me he was starting to show sighs of getting it as well.

"The last time I threatened to fire him, he said he was starting to like his martinis better shaken, not stirred anyway.

"I'm not sure if that meant he would go to work for MI6 or he was hooked on going to the movies, but for sick men, Major Tex and The Brit were laughing awfully hard in the background.

"To tell you the truth, I'm starting to look forward to our little chats. It's like getting addicted to a soap opera. Will the Seal Return?"

Dunn sat quietly with a big smile on his face then said, "Now if you would times that by two, then add about a billion, you might get close to the two problems I used to have," he informed everyone. "One time, when it looked like their Agency Fathers were set up, then assassinated, they pulled out all the stops."

"After leading me to believe they would let it go and not seek revenge, they recruited a clandestine logistical support group that included one of the Agency jets. People involved in other ongoing overseas clandestine activities helped them. They even got MI6 in Jamaica involved. If they hadn't by accident uncovered an international plot in the process, they would have been put into prison and I probably would have been put under the prison. They just have unbelievable luck."

"It was all very well planned out," Blue Jay defended.

"To the last detail," Bean added, but neither one could hold a straight face and started laughing.

"You laugh," Dunn said. "That nasty bitch from the State Department thought she had us by the short and curlies and was well on her way to making a big name for herself.

"Must admit though, I did enjoy taking her down a peg or two and getting rid of that asshole political general that was assigned to the Agency was a definite plus."

When everyone again had settled down, Jockey thought it was a good time to start the Bull Shit Derby. He walked up to the podium and started with, "Found these envelopes lying here," as he held them into the air.

"This one reads, To General Mac," he said, then opened it and started to read. "Mac may have winter in his hair, but he has summer in his heart. True, true," Jockey agreed, then continued to read. "If anything springs up, it will probably fall. Now that's just cruel," Jockey scolded.

"No problem, I've been shooting pool with a rope for years," Mac responded to the reading.

Jockey shook his head and smiled at Mac, as he picked up the other envelope. "Doesn't seem to be anything written on this one," he announced, as he opened it. After quickly reading it, he smiled. "Looks like we have all been invited to a wedding." He read the invitation. "You are all cordially invited to attend the marriage of our Not Worth a Shit Agency Son's to the Pecker Neck Sisters."

When the laughter quieted down, Jockey announced, "We know the IDs of the grooms, but who are the Pecker Neck Sisters?"

The Ladies didn't react right away, then Lady1 offered, "Whoever they are, I feel a great deal of sympathy for them. Can't even imagine what it would be like being married to dipshit and numb nuts."

"And let's not forget the father-in-laws and their obsessions with those old iron fragmentation grenades," LadyA added. "The way they handle them, I get the feeling they think they are iron boobies."

"I know what you mean," Lady1 agreed. "I guess the new brides could casually explain their father-in-laws were big in IBM. No one has to know it means Iron Boobie Magnets."

"Knew I liked these kids," Jar Head said, as he burst into laughter.

"They are all right!" Doggie agreed. "Maybe we should try to fix them up for real."

LadyA, Lady1, Bean, and Blue Jay immediately stood up, pointed at the two, and said in unison, "Don't get any ideas!"

"They would make lovely couples," Swabbie approved with a big smile and immediately came under a barrage of dinner rolls.

The Bull Shit Derby was again off to a rousing start and looked like it would surpass earlier Derbies.

The Derby went on longer than usual, but when it finally seemed to be slowing down, Jockey announced, "I guess it's time for the Annual JCCF Award part of the evening."

"Virtual Annual," Panda corrected.

"I again stand corrected by Panda, the politically correct dick wad. The Virtual Annual JCCF Award."

"What is a dick wad?" LadyA inquired.

"Going to go way out on a limb here, but I'm assuming you do know what a dick is?" Bean started to explain. "Well, if a man is wearing a pair of very tight pants, that's what you call the bulge in front, Dick Wad!"

LadyA looked at Bean who demonstrated someone throwing like a girl and she knew it was payback for her insinuating he threw like a girl, so she flipped him the bird. "I haven't noticed any like that around the Barn, have you, Lady1?"

"I'd rather not say," she replied. "I don't want to be the cause of a serious shortage due to people trying to fill the void with rolled up paper towels or knots tied in washcloths."

"YAR!" the Team all replied in unison, as everyone burst into laughter.

"What will tomorrow bring?" JJ inquired while still laughing.

"Knowing the Team, the area will probably resemble a logging camp," JC answered.

"Maybe I better go into the refrigerator tonight and put a lock on the vegetable compartment," Top suggested.

When things finally settled down, Jockey continued. "I will now read the current point standings and as in the past, ask you to hold your applause until the end. JC 6, Blue Jay 4¼, Benz 4, Bean 4, Panda 3, Check 2, Bris 1, Lady1 1, and Mac ½." Everyone gave mock applause.

"Before starting the presentation of the new points, I would like to say something. Shortly after the Team was formed in 2001, someone who shall remain anonymous," Jockey said, as he pointed directly at JC, "made a disparaging remark about my flying abilities and suggested that I learned how to fly at Pussy Airways. Others picked up on the humorous remark and one in particular seemed to take great delight in mentioning it from time to time and that brings us to our first presentation.

"Blue Jay, for being outmaneuvered, then scared by Peeka, minus ½ point!"

When everyone stopped laughing, Jockey continued. "I guess that falls under the category of 'What goes around, comes around' or in this case, 'What goes around, gets scared by the little pussy.'"

"Get stuffed!" was heard and as usual, another ½-point deduction was awarded for attacking the presenter and that brought the total to minus 1 point.

"JC, for putting himself into a very dangerous position and after being complimented by the terrorist leader for doing a good job on guard duty, took out the leader and another terrorist at close range. 1 Point!

"Blue Jay, after causing the destruction of a perfectly good martini shaker and expressing his intense dislike for wicker furniture, took out a very bad man in Jamaica, and almost got himself killed in the process. Again! 2 points!

"Benz and Panda, probably thinking a flame-thrower was going to be used for a weenie roast or something, took on four men with big knives, and after a furious fight, defeated them, 1½ points each. On second thought, maybe 1½ of those points should be virtual points."

"Stick the 1½ virtual points, where the sun virtually never shines," Panda suggested.

"And another minus ½ point is awarded," Jockey replied.

"This shit is fixed," Benz commented, then continued laughing.

"Benz and Panda, 1 point each," Jockey corrected, then added, "and I must say, I am shocked by all of these attacks on the presenter."

"Dick wad!" was a reply from an anonymous voice in the group who recently found out what it meant.

"Bean, AKA, Mr. Stealth, in spite of wasting two perfectly good grenades, managed to somehow delay the advanced unit pursuing the Team 2 points."

"Fuck face."

"One point!" were the immediate exchanges.

"Tic, after representing a terrorist bomber during a dispute with a train conductor and probably saving lives on the train, then making fast friends prior to neutralizing that terrorist, 1 point."

LadyA and Lady1, after chicken arm girl throws of two grenades that almost took them and everyone else on their side out, they beat back an attack from the left flank, 1 point each.

"Top Kiner, after drawing his pistol and taking out three bad people attacking from his right flank, 1 point. He was originally awarded 1½ points, but after it was discovered he spun the pistol on his index finger as he put it back into its holster and stated he wanted to be called, *The Top with No Name*, got a ¼ point deduction for doing cowboy shit during a firefight. Also got a ¼-point deduction for big spoon activity in the kitchen. I'm not sure what that last part means, but I'll be sure to get a clarification.

"Pru and Met, for continued excellent long-range shooting for over 7 years, 1 point each. The secret committee also realized it is a hard job to both shoot and carry those heavy weapons around, so they have recommended you be given some help. Since they couldn't line up a shit coolie, they settled for the next best thing and suggested Panda handle the drag bags from now on. The privilege also goes with the new codename of Panda the Coolie or Coolie Panda whichever works for you."

"Eat shit."

"An automatic ½ point deduction will be made to any future awards to Panda," was the immediate announcement.

"The Board for their ingenuity and resourcefulness when problems were encountered with the pulley system, getting the fuel to shore, and setting up for refueling, 3 ½ points!"

"Then that would be ½ point per Board member?" Mac inquired.

"Half a point each," Jockey quickly replied, as he checked the sheet of paper in front of him for the next item.

"Then that takes my total from ½ point to 1 point and no longer the lowest."

"That's correct," Jockey answered, wondering why Mac was asking these questions.

"Then I guess with now having the lowest point total, the other Board members are in line for the prestige LBJ 'Is that guy sucking hind tit award' or will it now be 'Are those guys sucking hind tit award.'"

"Shit, I didn't think about that," Jockey said in a low voice. "I'll have to check with the secret committee about that. Will send out a special and our fastest secret carrier pigeon right after the presentations."

"I told you it was all fixed," Benz called to Mac.

"I always knew it, but just didn't want to admit it. I want to register a complaint," Mac announced and the entire Team yelled, "YAR!"

"Ah, hell, we'll accept the award," Wilson spoke up. "We feel it wouldn't be fair giving it to Mac since he already looks like a hind tit. On second thought, just spray him with plaster of paris and we'll stand him up in a corner of the boardroom." With that, the other Board members all yelled, "YAR!"

Wilson then looked at Mac and said, "Peeka told me about the name of the toy you made for her."

Mac laughed and raised his glass toward Wilson who did the same in return.

Jockey was laughing hard, but then regrouped and yelled, "At ease, at ease, all you unruly buccaneers."

"The Team, House Team, Board, Jar Head, Doggie, Swabbie, for your participation in the last Project and one hell of a firefight, 1 point each."

Everyone was waiting for the usual punch line, but it didn't come and everyone saw that Jockey was serious.

"I hope you gave yourself 2 points," JC said in a loud voice. Everyone yelled, "YAR!" in agreement and for the first time since they had known him, Jockey was at a loss for words.

After he recovered, Jockey said, "Now for the totals"

JC 8, Blue Jay 6¼, Benz 6, Bean 6, Panda 5, Check 3, Bris 2, Mac 2, Tic 2, Pru 2, Met 2, Top 2, LadyA 2, Lady1 3, JJ 1½, Dunn 1½, Wilson 1½, Dawson 1½, Howard 1½, Foxie 1½, and Jockey 2."

As usual, the party was going into the wee hours of the morning. It was a good thing they were in the country because every once in a while, the noise almost made the Barn shake.

This was one of the very few times the Team let their guard down. Not totally, but enough to unwind and enjoy themselves.

Even if they were fully alert, it would not have mattered because it would have been almost impossible to detect this expert in stealth movement moving silently toward the area where all of the noise was coming from. Down the hall on wood floors without making a sound, then after a pause, slipped into the party area without even being noticed until Top finally exclaimed, "Peeka!" as he moved his chair back from the table.

She knew that was an invitation and immediately jumped onto his lap. After a quick sign of affection, she started scanning the goodies on the table.

"She wants to join the party," JJ observed.

"It's that or *you woke me up, now feed me,*" Mac added with a smile.

"Did you miss us while we were away?" Top inquired.

"Ho, yeah," the wives of Jar Head, Doggie, and Swabbie all agreed. "Every day, she would check the house, then the Barn. Sometimes she would disappear. We would go looking for her and find her sleeping on one of the beds upstairs in the Barn."

Everyone looked at her and Peeka knew she was the center of attraction, as she rubbed against Top and gave everyone blinkie eyes.

Some time later, everyone was finally partied out and it was getting around the time when that question was usually asked, so everyone listened up when Jar Head asked, "What do you people think about the big picture on fighting terrorism?"

"I thought it would be better, but it seems the terrorists have been allowed to regroup and re-train," JC started, "and these last few Projects prove they are on the comeback and we are still needed."

"My feelings about the Al-Qaida situation are if they are allowed to continue to be left alone because they are in Pakistan, they will just get stronger and the next attack will make 9/11 look like a minor event," Mac added. "As for Iraq, Al-Sadr is Iran's man. That so-called government in Iraq let him run free in the beginning, now they can't control him and he is just waiting until we pull out, then his militia will take over the country."

"My opinion about the military on that topic is it's an as usual situation," Dunn spoke up. "We get into a war, the peace time political generals and admirals are in command, can't handle the job when it comes to conducting a war, and until they were replaced, things weren't good. Past examples of that are the Union forces during the Civil War. The North had the material and men, but the South was getting the upper hand until generals like Grant, Sherman, and others took command. World War Two had Admiral Nimitz and other com-manders.

"I only hope Generals Petraeus and Odierno are the Grant and Sherman type commanders that get the job done.

"It has taken a lot longer than before, but Lincoln and Roosevelt were good presidents trying to solve a problem.

"Today, we have a president that, among other things, has developed a new math. One Plus one equals whatever I say it equals, and it's usually wrong."

Everyone chuckled then the room again got quiet until JJ stood up and broke the silence. "I would like to say something that concerns things closer to home. I was the one who had the idea about this group and want to again thank you all for joining me.

"Sometimes wish I hadn't formed the group, especially when you all are sent into harm's way. It's not as bad when I am with you, but from a distance it's different.

"My opinion is society seems to think or want to think that since things have quieted down, there is no longer a major threat, but we all know that isn't the case. Just under the surface, things haven't quieted down and if the terrorists are allowed to get stronger, society will have a rude awakening.

"I would like to continue and hope you all feel the same, but will understand if anyone would not like to continue." JJ then sat down and pulled his chair closer to the table.

When he looked up, everyone was standing with glass in hand raised in his direction telling him they were all still with him.

Have gone on ahead to perform Recon:

Lt. Col. Dermott McDonald USMC

Mr. Andy Domingo

Mr. Howard Powers

Peeka